RESPECT

The Best Revenge is Success

notionpress.com

RESPECT

The Best Revenge is Success

DAVY MOHAN

notionpress.com

Notion Press

Old No. 38, New No. 6

McNichols Road, Chetpet

Chennai - 600 031

First Published by Notion Press 2015

ISBN 978-93-5206-501-1

Contents

Acknowledgements

I would like to thank GOD for his provisions and blessings.

I would like to express my gratitude to the many people who saw me through this book – to all those who provided support, talked things over, read, wrote, offered comments, allowed me to quote their remarks and assisted in the editing, proofreading and design.

I would like to thank Notion Press for their support in publishing this book. Above all I want to thank my wife, Roshni, and the rest of my family, who supported and encouraged me in spite of all the time it took me away from them. It was a long and difficult journey for them.

1. Where It Ends

The room is dark and gloomy, with just some light filtering in through the open balcony door. The sun begins its descent; darkness waits to claim the room. I am sitting on the only chair in the room, with a glass of whiskey in my hand. As I gaze at the sun, I suddenly begin to laugh loudly – much to everyone's astonishment. I feel a hand on my shoulder. It is Ghoush Khan, my trusted aide and friend.

"Where are they?" I ask.

"They are on their way."

As I walk out onto the large balcony, a strong wind blows the curtains aside. Khan follows me.

"Finally, Khan! Now, I will be able to sleep in peace. It took some time, but it is finally done."

Khan nods. As I stand there, I turn and see my reflection in a glass panel in the window. Thick beard, wrinkled face, long wavy hair, blue Armani suit, Gucci boots, stained teeth...I look like a monster. I see another image taking form in the glass panel next to me. It is an image of me from a decade ago. Clean-shaven, short hair, neatly dressed... Ten years of a bitter, vengeful journey has made me look like what I am now. Back then, life was simple.

Was all this worth it? I had dedicated the last decade of my life to this one purpose. Now what? I begin to think back to how it all started. Khan refills my glass. I shout, "Khan! Get more ice and another bottle from the car. I will be staying here tonight." He quietly goes to the inner room and instructs the boys.

2. The Past

I was born into a respected Bengali family. My father had studied in IIT Chennai. We had a big house in the heart of Bangalore. My family comprised of my father, mother, brother and me. Dad, a smart businessman and owned a block-manufacturing factory. We enjoyed all the luxuries of life. We had a horde of servants and drivers around the house – in the 1980s, labour was cheap and loyalty lasted longer.

One day, dad came home from work, earlier than usual.

Mom asked him, "Are you okay? You don't look too well. Have you taken your medicines?"

"I don't want to take those damn medicines. I feel sleepy and can't concentrate," dad replied.

"But Dr. Prakash specifically asked you to take those tablets so that we can avoid another incident," mom replied.

While I was trying to listen to them, my mother turned around and said, "Aryan, leave the room and take Dev along with you." Her voice was cold and firm. So, I picked up my brother and left. I could hear screams and shouts coming from the room, followed by the sound of crying. After a while, they emerged from the bedroom. Victory gleamed on my mother's face. We sat down for lunch and enjoyed delicious mutton biryani and chicken kebabs. After lunch, a small box of tablets was pushed towards dad. He looked at them with disgust. He reached for the contents of the box and swallowed it all in one gulp. Then, he picked up a glass of water and drank it.

"Dad, what are those tablets for?" I asked.

"Vitamins," I got the answer from my mother, who was in the kitchen. Dad maintained his disgruntled look.

My brother and I attended St. Florence, a school located close to our neighbourhood. It had a good reputation for sports and extracurricular activities. We were dropped off and picked up by our driver in our new, red Maruti car. I was a very quiet and reserved person; always ate my lunch alone, away from the crowd. No one bothered me and I didn't take part in any of the games they played during the break. It was a quiet life, except for the little episodes of dad's sickness that showed up now and then. Though mom tried to hide dad's sickness from us, I almost always knew. I soon figured out why dad was having those tablets – he had seizures. I guess Dev knew, but he lived in denial.

As the years passed, dad's sickness became more serious, and the seizures became more frequent. Business also took a hit. The drivers were dismissed, and Dev and I were put into a shared auto for the trip to school. This was a three-wheeled vehicle, with at least 10 to 12 kids shoved inside. It had a small handle bar, fixed at the entrance of the vehicle, as a token of safety. That pitiful rod, put there to protect us from falling outside, still has me laughing. Soon, all the servants were let go and we had to help out with the chores in the house.

One day, I overheard my uncles speaking to dad.

"Brother, we think you should shut down the factory. Your health does not permit you to take care of your business. We can't keep leaving our jobs to come and help you every time you get sick."

I stood behind the door, where they couldn't see me or the tears welling up in my eyes. Losers! It was because of my grandfather's and dad's help that these relatives were well settled in life. Now, we were a burden to them. I could see my mom standing in the corner, quietly listening to them.

After they left, dad asked mom, "What do you think, dear? Am I a burden to you all? Should I shut down the factory and sit at home?"

Mom cleared the table and walked into the other room. She came back later with a small book in her hand. She opened the pages and showed it to my dad and then told him. "This is all we have. There is no option other than to get a regular job or sell the factory. You decide. I am behind you." Dad laughed, "Don't worry, it's all cool." Those words ring a bell even now.

One night, at 2a.m., my mother shook me awake. As I got up in shock, she gestured that I should not scream or make noise, as Dev was sleeping next to me. I got up and followed her into the other room. Dad was lying on the floor, shaking violently.

"Mom, why did you wake me up for this? You know he will be okay in a while," I asked, half-asleep.

"Aryan, this is his fourth attack tonight. I have spoken to the doctor and he has prescribed a medicine that needs to be given to your dad immediately."

"But mom, its 2a.m! Which medical shop will be open now?"

"There is one on Cunningham Road called Cash Pharmacy that is open 24 hrs."

"Okay, call Teja uncle. We can ask him to go get the medicines."

"After all the nonsense they said to your dad, you still want to ask them for help?"

"Then how are we going to get the medicines?"

This was the 1980s. Bangalore came to a standstill by 10p.m., except for a few mischievous souls who wandered the streets.

"Aryan, you will have to go," she said. I was shocked, and wondered if the lady had lost her mind. I was 10 years old and had never stepped outside my house any time later than 5p.m. While I was engrossed in my thoughts, she dumped the money and prescription in my hand and told me to get it soon. I was pushed out of the door, still in my nightclothes. As I walked down the stairs, I was worried, scared and frightened. The thoughts of the graveyard close by came to my mind. All the horror movie climaxes began to replay in my head. I nervously looked around, to see if I could spot the lady in a white sari holding a candle. There was pin-drop silence.

The destination was at least 5 km away. I needed some kind of protection. I picked up the spike tool that was used to loosen the garden soil. I felt some sort of comfort with the tool in my hand. As I walked onto the main road, my mom's words echoed in my mind: "Get it soon." How this was going to happen 'soon' was beyond my understanding. It would take at least an hour to get it and come back. I began to run, when I suddenly heard the noise of a vehicle behind me. I turned around and saw a beam of light coming towards me. Without thinking twice, I jumped in front of the vehicle – a Luna (a small two-wheeler). It screeched to a halt as the front wheel of the vehicle lodged itself right in between my legs. The elderly man on the bike was as startled as I was. We stared at each other for some time. Our eyes locked; he wanted to shout at me, but was still looking for the right curse words. I acted first by holding the spike tool to his neck. He swallowed his words and meekly asked me, "What do you want?"

"Take me to Cunningham Road and back. I need to buy medicines for my dad," I said.

He was surprised but after a couple of seconds, he told me to get on to his vehicle. I kept the spike raised, close to his neck.

"You're just a kid," he muttered.

"A kid with a knife," I replied.

"That's not a knife," he said and started the bike.

I could feel him tremble, but I didn't know if it was from fear or the cold. I didn't care. We reached the pharmacy. I walked in and woke up the pharmacists by shouting, "EXCUSE ME! ANYONE HERE?" A man popped up from behind the counter, adjusted his pants and asked,

"What do you want?"

"Masala dosa!" I replied sarcastically. "Medicines!" I quickly thrust the prescription into his hands. He looked at me quizzically and asked, "You have come alone?"

I replied, "Look, my uncle is on the bike outside."

"Oh. Let me get the medicines for you."

While he was looking for the medicines, I removed the money from my pocket. My hands were steady. My thoughts were broken by the sound of the Luna speeding away. The pharmacist brought the medicines and gave them to me. "105 rupees," he said with his hands held out. I was handing over the money to him, when he looked up and noticed that the Luna had disappeared.

"Hey! Where is your uncle?" he asked while reaching out to grab the medicines.

I slammed the money on the table with one hand and removed the spike with the other. "Let go of the bag! Take the money and let the bag go!"

I ran back home with the tablets and spike. Later on, I learnt from some people in school that those tablets had a very high dosage of nerve relaxants – it was the kind of thing that most drug addicts used to get high.

Life went on. Dad's seizures worsened; whenever he had one of his episodes, Dev was sent out of the room and I stayed on as dad writhed on the floor. There was nothing much one could do, other than wait and clear the surroundings of sharp objects. Sometimes, the attacks came so suddenly that he would fall down with a loud thud and hit his head on the table, chair or toilet closet. His head would cut open and blood would be spattered everywhere. The sad part was that we could not do anything until he regained consciousness. I was too thin and small to lift my dad's body. The most I was able to do was to place his head on my lap, and press ice cubes, wrapped in a towel, on his wounds. My pants would be soaked with my father's blood. Eventually, the bleeding would reduce. My mother and I would then nurse the wounds and help him get to bed, where he would pass out.

Soon, Dev and I had to shift to a school that better suited our budget. We enrolled at St. Andrews High School. It was how I had pictured prison to be. Absolute, total mayhem. Mom tried to explain to our nosy relatives that the decision to shift schools was taken because it was closer to home and taught Hindi as a second language. I could see her trying to make justifications to people, but I knew the real reason. We were well on our way to being flat out broke. Dev didn't have a clue though. The poor fellow didn't know what went on in the house most of the time. He was the friendly sort of guy, the kind everybody took notice of. Whenever he entered a room filled with people, he always left with a friend.

An unfortunate thing about belonging to a rich family was that, even after we were broke, we still needed to maintain the image of being rich. Ha! I wish there was a special quota for people like us.

Life in the new school began. I was my quiet self, and continued to eat lunch with Dev. Dev made many friends quickly, but he would come and sit with me during lunch break. One day, I told him that he didn't have to join me for lunch anymore. The next day, I was eating my lunch alone in the playground. The playground hosted five football matches, two hockey matches and two cricket matches concurrently during lunchtime. I wondered how the boys were able to distinguish who their teammates were and which ball belonged to their team as everyone wore the same uniform. There were incidents when a guy from one group would kick a ball of another group's into the goal and begin to cheer for himself and demand a hug from his team mates, until he realised he had kicked a ball in the goal from another group. Sometimes the entire ground would break into laughter, but most of the time it would end in a scuffle. Everyone seemed to be having fun, except for one particular guy who would walk up to the centre of the field everyday and begin to pray, in spite of all the balls whizzing past him. I suppose he wanted the balls to knock some sense into him.

One day, during recess, I was walking down the corridor, lunch bag in hand, when someone pushed me against the wall. I looked up and saw that it was Philip, also known as 'THE CLASS BULLY'. He yelled in my face, "I challenge you to a W.W.F match!" During those days, watching and imitating W.W.F matches, which originated in the USA, was a craze among schoolboys. They would try to emulate their dressing and behaviour. Here, they created their own local version, by wearing their ties around their heads instead of around the collar. I looked at him and said, "No". He threw me against the wall and marched up to me. Within seconds there was a SNAP! The noise was that of a bone breaking. Pin-drop silence followed. Philip's cries echoed in the corridor a few seconds later. Everybody looked at me in disbelief. As I recollected, I had lifted him up and slammed him down on the floor. The bone in his arm had snapped as he had fallen down on his arm. The school nurse was summoned and Philip was rushed to the hospital. Meanwhile, the teacher asked all the children there as to what had happened, but all they got in response was complete silence. Prison rules applied here as well. Everyone was warned and sent back to their respective classes. A couple of days later, Philip came back to class. The teacher entered our 6th standard 'B' classroom and asked Philip to reveal who was responsible for the fracture. His reply: "I fell down."

During lunch break, I got up and walked out of class. Philip came in front of me again. Thoughts began to race in my mind. He smiled and placed his hand (the one that was not fractured) on my shoulder. "You are thin, but quite strong. Come, let's have lunch together." Out of guilt, I agreed. That particular lunch with him changed my image from a silent, reserved boy to a tough one within minutes. The entire 6th standard knew my name and everything there was to know about me. In the days that followed, I was treated like a king among the boys. They offered me their lunch, and bought me ice cream, samosas and cool drinks.

Life, school and people slowly became interesting to me. I steadily became popular among the juniors as well as the seniors. Once in a while, a few kids became my scapegoats in order to instill fear in others but all was good. I was known as the 'infamous Aryan Dutt'. In almost all of the school literary fests and sports meets, I would represent the school for some activity. After having established a name for myself in my school, I decided to target other schools by bullying the boys there. Over time, I made a name for myself among them as well. I would walk into any of the school auditoriums with my friends and the boys would immediately move out of their seats to give us their seats. Our gang became famous. This caused a lot of mayhem in our school, to the extent that boys from some other schools pooled in their pocket money and hired a goon to beat some sense into us. However, he was our friend – an old school senior. He collected money from them, and turned around and belted them instead of us. The story became famous. We started taking money from the boys in exchange for protection. We considered ourselves a smaller version of the mafia. We used the money to indulge in cigarettes and liquor. I never had to carry money. Things were brought and given to me. In fact, the school blazer, which only a few fortunate souls in my school could buy, was given to me by my classmates whenever I went to other schools to represent ours. I was elected the literary president out of sheer popularity. I was living the 'good life' at least in school.

Dad finally decided to sell the factory machinery. We hardly had any money in hand, and whatever we had saved had begun to dwindle. Naryan, my dad's factory supervisor, found a broker who was willing to help us sell the factory machinery. They managed to find a buyer – Capco Blocks Pvt Ltd, run by Mr. Arun, dad's only rival at that time. Dad requested us to sell it to anyone else but him. However, mom convinced him that food on the table was much more important than pride, and that they were the highest bidder we had found. Mr. Arun's only demand was that my dad should come to collect the cash. So, dad, my uncle and I went to sell the machinery. When we entered the factory office, we were asked to wait at the reception area. While waiting, tears began to well up in dad's eyes for the first time in his life. He cried silently. The peon directed us into the office. I asked my dad and uncle to wait outside in the reception area and I went into the office room. The owner asked me, "Where is your father?"

"He is outside."

"You are?"

"I am his older son."

"Good. Which class are you studying in?"

"Why? Are you planning on paying my fees?"

He was surprised at my rude response – as surprised as I was. I guess something inside me had broken after having seen my father cry for the first time.

"At one time, your dad was my only competitor – that is why I am paying extra for the outdated crap you are selling to me," he said.

"That outdated crap is at your entrance gate. Pay up," I replied.

He swiftly took the cash out and slammed it on the table.

"The money is here. Twenty thousand rupees. Where is your father, as per our agreement?"

"I am changing the agreement. Give me the money. Take the outdated crap and let us go, or we will just leave. You can keep the money too. My family is used to donating to beggars."

He threw the money at me and shouted in anger, "Take your father and get out of here!"

I smiled at him, stood up, took the money and left. Unlike Amitabh Bachchan in the movies, I did not have the option of leaving the wad of notes there. On the way back, there was total silence in the car. I asked my uncle and dad not to tell anyone what had happened in there. That evening, I drank alone on my terrace. I vowed revenge, no matter how long it would take. I did not tell any of my friends what had happened. None of them even knew about my dad's condition. Hurt and anger was brewing as a dangerous concoction within me.

3. Engineer or Doctor?

Time flew by and life went on as usual. When I finished my 12th standard exams, the usual debate of engineer or doctor began in my family. Like most South Indian boys, I had only two options back then – to become either a doctor or an engineer. There was a heated discussion among the elders in my extended family on how many doctors we had in comparison to engineers. Since my dad was an engineer, I was destined to become one as per the South Indian genetics code.

My dad, the only sensible one, asked me, "What do you say, Aryan? What do you want to become?"

Several pairs of eyes were staring at me, waiting to brand me as a rogue or a disciplined boy. I muttered, "Architect." (I had heard lots of girls took up that course, and decided that if I was going to have to live in hell, it might as well be beautiful.) The relatives were happy with my response; truth was, they didn't have a clue as to what I really wanted to do.

Dad replied, "That is a good choice, but it is a five-year course. I don't think you have the patience for that. Why not civil engineering? It is almost the same thing."

Those words sealed my fate. How could I explain to dad that, after spending 18 years in a boys' school and college, I needed to interact with the 'other kind'. Civil engineering was a subject that guys usually picked. Which girl in her right mind would like to mix concrete and play with sand during her practicals?

"Sure dad," I replied. I could not turn him down. Mom wanted me to do computer science. That was something I hated, so I ignored her request completely. I did not want her request to come on to the voting list. Soon the verdict came out, and I applied for civil engineering. My real desire was to do business and make money. I decided that until I figured out what business I wanted to get into, I would add an engineering title to my name. Only an engineer would truly understand what I had to go through to become one. I always imagined college life to be peaceful – what lay in store was an eye opener. I got selected into Ms Ramaiah Engineering College, Civil Branch. On the very first period of the first day, I was thrown out of class for chatting – rather, trying to initiate a conversation – with the guy sitting in front of me. While walking down the corridor, I thought to myself that this was going to be a long four years. While I was thinking and walking, my head held down, someone ran straight into me. We both fell down. I got up, dusted myself and caught hold of the other guy's collar. Shockingly, he caught my collar too.

"Hey asshole! Can't you watch where you are running?" I asked.

"Hey asshole, why did you have to come in my way while I was running?" he replied.

We burst out laughing.

"Hi! I'm Aryan."

"I'm Sahail."

"Which year, Sahail?"

"First year civil," he replied. "What about you?"

"First year civil."

"What are you doing out of class?"

"Professor threw me out."

Sahail laughed and walked towards class. "Catch you later, buddy. I am already late."

"Sure. Come to the canteen when you get thrown out. I will be waiting for you," I replied.

"No way. See you in the second period," he said.

I decided to head home and try out college another day. Just then, I felt a hand on my shoulder. It was Sahail. I didn't ask him what or why; I just laughed and he joined in. We soon became thick friends. He was from Jammu – one of those fair-skinned, handsome guys that girls run after. He was the son of a powerful minister. His apartment soon became our adda (hangout); we would bunk classes and chill out there. His pet name was 'Emran Hashmi' (Bollywood star). He was juggling at least three girlfriends at the same time – the funny thing was that all the girls knew about the others. He was like a trophy – they just had to have him. The girls even tried setting me up with their friends so that they would be one up on the competition. However, I stayed away from all this drama. I enjoyed my drinks, music and the mutton that Sahail's cook prepared specially for me.

One day, Sahail came up to me, looking worried and perplexed. "The seniors asked me not to speak to Anjali."

"Why?" I asked.

"Some senior called Pratap is interested in her," Sahail replied.

"So what? You continue to do what you want. They can't do anything."

"Aryan, I am not from these parts. These are local fellows and our seniors."

I caught his hand and asked him to point out the boy who had asked him to stay away from her. "There! That fat fellow and his friends near the canteen."

I took him to the bike stand and asked him to take out his bike.

"Why?"

"Shut up and do as I say. How much cash do you have on you?"

"Two hundred bucks."

"More than enough. Come."

We went to Guru Bar, near college. It was 11 in the morning. We walked up to the counter and asked the guy for a quarter and a pack of cigarettes. "Rs. 110."

"Pay him, Sahail."

We sat down at the plastic table, which was provided by the generous owner who encouraged guys like us who started so early in the day.

"Here," I poured Sahail a drink.

"Are you crazy? It's 11 in the morning!"

"Shut up and drink."

After we finished the drinks, we rode back to college.

Sahail kept insisting that we go back to the apartment. I said, "No. We have a small account to settle."

We went to the college canteen. I spotted the seniors from a distance. I walked up to the fat fellow and tapped him on the shoulder. He turned around and asked, "What do you want?"

"Sahail, this is the fellow, right?"

"Yeah, Aryan."

"Sahail, please ask him to repeat what he asked you not to do," I said loudly.

"Could you repeat what you had asked of me?"

By this time, the entire group surrounded us; they realised that we were drunk.

The fat fellow began to stammer, "No...boss, I just told him...don't talk to girls in college. Do whatever you want outside..."

"Why, you fat fart? Did her father hire you as her bodyguard?" I asked him.

The people gathered around us began to laugh.

From the crowd, someone spoke: "I sent him."

I turned around and saw a guy sitting on the table, his legs resting on the chair.

"My name is Pratap," he said, then jumped off the table and started walking towards me.

I began to laugh, and Sahail joined in. The guy was barely 5 feet and 3 inches tall.

I grabbed him by his collar and asked him, "Why? Is she your sister?"

"Hey, leave my collar! I am an ACP's son. Leave me! I am warning you..." Before he could finish speaking, there was a 'whack' – the noise made by my hand as it came in contact with his cheek. He fell flat on the floor. The entire crowd was silent. I said, "I am letting you go this time. Forget that girl and find yourself another girl of your height, Chottu. This is my college and that is my friend. If you get your father involved in this, I will hunt you down and reduce your height by another six inches." Not one of his batch mates or friends came forward. I could see that they were happy someone had dared to teach 'Chottu' a lesson.

I walked away from him and stared at the fat fellow.

"Sorry, bhai! I didn't know who you were," the fat fellow muttered.

Sahail and I bought more booze and celebrated our victory. The girl, for whom the battle was fought, came to his apartment and spent the night with him. I sat alone in the balcony, thinking to myself: *Who would that one girl be, who would earn my respect?* Looking at the number of girls that kept walking into Sahail's apartment daily, I wondered if there were any decent girls left in college.

Life went on. After that day, none of the seniors bothered us. In fact, they became quite friendly and helped us out when teachers created problems for us. Even Chottu became friendly with us. He would say, "For three years, no one ever dared to call me Chottu. You entered college, and now everyone calls me Chottu!"

"Out of love, out of love," I replied.

One evening, at Najji's Bakery, I was drinking a glass of cold milk and puffing on a cigarette, when I noticed a group of girls who were waiting for their turn at the STD booth. Among them was a girl with short hair; she was wearing an oversized leather jacket and spectacles, and was laughing and chatting with the others. I was in a daze – so much so that I didn't notice Sahail was standing next to me. Suddenly, he clapped his hands and broke my reverie. I looked at him, irritated, and asked, "What?"

"When did you become normal?" he asked

"What do mean?"

"Since when did you start getting interested in women?"

Oh shit! He noticed! I thought to myself.

"Why are you blushing, macho man?" he asked.

"Nothing! You are mistaken. There is nothing, yaar."

"Okay Aryan, at least tell me who it is. I will stop bugging you."

"The leather jacket," I said hesitantly.

He turned around, looked at her and began to laugh. "Out of all the girls in college, you like that one?"

"Why? What's wrong with her?"

"She is a total geek. Full scholarship material. She looks hot, but is not interested in any guy. Manju tried his luck with her; she struck him down on his first approach. Secondly, she is in computer science."

"Have you tried your stunts with her?" I asked

"Me? Bhai, I go with the easy-come-easy-go type. I don't run after these complicated structures. They are bad for health," he replied.

"The ones you fool around with are bad for your wealth," I said.

"Wealth is not a problem; my dad has plenty. Peace of mind and health – that's really important. Now, let's get back to the apartment. I need to pick up my 'peace of mind' from the hostel." He winked at me and started the bike.

"Carry on. I am going back home today. I will see you in college tomorrow."

"Don't do anything stupid, Aryan," He shouted as he rode off.

The girls turned around and looked at me. I slowly slid the cigarette down and stubbed it out with my foot. They went back to chatting among themselves. I started my bike.

"Bhai! See you tomorrow," some of the seniors standing nearby shouted when I removed my bike from the parking lot. I nodded at them and sped away.

4. Examination Scam

On the home front, we had almost exhausted the family's savings. Dad was in a near vegetative state. He moved around, but rarely talked. He couldn't register any new information; sometimes, he even forgot which branch of engineering I was studying. I couldn't really blame the old man – the sedatives he was taking kept him in a dazed state for long periods of time. He was there, but not all there in this mind. Such a brilliant mind, but something was holding him back. Seeing him in that state, I used to shed tears. He never attended any of my school or award functions. I would tell myself that it was not his fault – it was as if he had given up on life. It was not as if he had drunk himself to this situation or gone mad during business failure. I remembered him from our younger days, when he was active and strong. *Life could really beat down the strongest among us*, I thought.

"Aryan, we need to sell the factory land," Mom said to me one day.

"I know...but is there any other way?" I asked.

"No, I don't think so. We need the money for Dev's college admission."

"Why don't we rent out the rear portion of the house, where the servants' quarters is located? It is vacant."

"What? Rent out the rear portion! Aren't you ashamed to even think of it?"

"Yes, I am ashamed mom, but I'd rather have money in my pocket than worry about being ashamed. It is time we moved on from family royalty and came down to where we actually stand in life. The rear portion of the property has access to the main road, so we can rent it for commercial purposes," I argued.

Mom agreed. Soon, the word spread people started approaching us. Mom had a strict screening test, which included the following conditions:

1. No compromises on the rent – not even a single paisa. The rent was fixed at Rs. 20,000.
2. The agreement was for a year, after which it had to be renewed.
3. Interested parties would have to bear expenses such as registration, lawyer fees, etc.
4. People known to us were preferred.

The list went on and on, and was changed according to the circumstances. I wondered if she would actually ever allow the place to be given on rent. Mom suddenly became bolder and outspoken. I asked her one day, "Ma, why are you so rigid?"

"This is all we have left. I want the best rate and no problematic party. With this money, I need to make sure both Dev and you are educated and well settled."

"Ma, we can't plan so much. Problems come and go. Don't worry; it's all going to be cool."

"Stop imitating your father. Look at what happened to Mr. Cool!"

I kept quiet. She was like a tigress protecting her cubs. I was called to sit with her for meetings with new prospects.

Dev was, as usual, kept away from all this. Lucky fellow – the realities of life had not hit him yet. I was happy for him.

At college, a few weeks after I had seen the girl in the leather jacket, I was introduced to her by a common friend. Her name was Sanjanna Rao.

"Hi, I am Aryan."

"Yes, I know. I have heard about you."

Shit! What story had she heard? I hesitantly asked her, "Where..." Before I could finish, she said, "You are the junior that beat up the senior right?"

"Oh, Chottu and I are good friends. We were just playing around!"

"Please. I have seen how the seniors respect you. You certainly must have done something to command such weight with the seniors."

"Hi! I am Sahail!" The idiot suddenly butted into our conversation. How I wished I had not met this fellow at all! Was he going to ruin my chance or was he trying to take a shot at this girl? Before I realised what was happening, she shook hands with Sahail and began to walk away.

"Ass! Why did you have to interfere at the wrong moment?"

"Bhai, you should have seen your face while you were talking to her. You looked like a puppy in love!" he laughed. "If she picked that up, it would be the end of your love story! Look at the authority with which she was grilling you. She is a nutcase; everyone knows that. You must be a fool to go after her."

In my mind, she was the girl who knew what I was capable of and still stood up to me. Gutsy girl.

Both the exams and the deal that fulfilled mom's criteria were forced upon me. The deal was for a restaurant. I was in a total dilemma as to whether I should study or concentrate on the deal. We had to handle the deal properly – if not, it could go haywire. Mom was on a power trip and would not budge on her demands, so I had to be the mediator-cum-agent. I was sitting in the bakery near college, wondering about my exams, when I was interrupted.

"Kya bhai, looks like you are in deep thought?" It was Chottu.

"Yaar, exams are on my head, and I haven't started studying. I am confused about what to do."

"Buy the question paper! Why are you worrying so much?"

"What? Can you arrange for the question paper?"

"Yes bhai. Which subjects do you need? Tell me and I will arrange them for you. But it will cost you."

"Cost? How much?"

"Rs. 15,000 per paper."

"What! Who has that kind of money? I will have to kidnap you and ask your father for that money!"

He gave me a disgruntled look. "I am trying to help you, and you're planning to screw me!"

"Arey yaar! I was joking. How am I going to arrange so much money?"

"Sell the paper to others, and you can make more money than your investment. Think about it and tell me."

I went to Sahail's apartment in the evening. "What do you think?" I asked him after telling him about my conversation with Chottu.

"As far as I know, bhai, I have not studied and I am going to fail. I can say the same applies for you. So, let's try this."

"What if we get caught while selling the paper? Or the paper turns out to be a fake?"I asked

"That is something we will worry about at that time. Now, let's get the paper."

I met Chottu later that night, with Sahail.

"Chottu, how trustworthy is this contact of yours?"

"Bhai! How do you think I reached final year?" He laughed.

"Okay, how is it done?" I asked him.

"Well, the night before the exam, around midnight, he will hand over one xerox copy of the question paper and collect his money. After that, you can make copies of the paper and sell it to whoever you want," Chottu said.

"If he gives it to us around 12, how are we to distribute the papers? When will we study?" I asked.

"Bhai! Give one copy to one of the nerds in your class and ask him to solve all the short questions and write down the answers for you to mug up. After distributing the paper, you can come back and study for 50 marks. You need only 35 to pass right? Are you trying to get first rank?" he replied.

"What an idea!" Sahail shouted.

"Chottu, What if the paper given at the exam is different? What then?" I asked.

"Bhai, I have not faced any problems till now. They are a 100 percent-genuine party," he replied.

"Will he give the money back if the papers are not genuine?" I asked.

"Okay. I will speak to my guy and ask him to give you the paper, and collect the money only after the exam. Is that okay?"

"Done," I replied.

Sahail and I left and went back to the apartment. We needed to arrange the cash for six subject papers – a total of Rs. 90,000. It was an unthinkable, unattainable amount for a college kid. As we wondered about what to do, Sahail got a call from his friend, who was studying in R.B. College of Engineering. He was enquiring about how Sahail's preparations were going, which textbooks he was studying from, and so on.

Sahail casually asked him, "How much would you pay if I could get you the question papers?"

"What? You got the papers? Please, brother, give it to me! I need it. My parents want me to get a distinction. I am under a lot of pressure. I will give you Rs. 3,000 for each. Please help me out."

"Calm down. I don't have any paper with me. Was just wondering, idiot!" Sahail replied.

There was silence at the other end of the line. Then he said, "Please, don't joke at times like this. Goodnight." He put the phone down.

Sahail related the entire incident to me. Chottu's idea struck like lightning. I explained to Sahail that, if we got even five people like his friend, we would be able to get one paper for free. We made a list of potential buyers. Three clients were from our college and two others from another college. We spoke to them and negotiated a price. The only problem was that some needed only electrical science, some need math and electrical science and some needed physics in addition to the other two. We decided to include more guys from different colleges. We soon had enough money to buy three papers; the other three papers were easy to pass.

So we decided to buy three subject papers and decided to get help for the other three from Arvind, the nerd in our class. He agreed to teach us enough to pass and to prepare for the 50-mark answer sheet for the other three subjects, as long as we supplied the question papers to him for free. It was all set. Soon, four colleges were involved and the number of people who wanted the papers increased. Marketing, bargaining, outsourcing and distribution – I learnt my very first business lesson through this paper scam.

This gave me the breathing space I needed in order to concentrate on closing the rental deal for the family. My days before the exam were spent running between the lawyers' office, xerox shops and Arvind's room in the hostel. We even borrowed a xerox machine from one of the rich guys to make copies of the papers, as the number of people had drastically increased.

Chottu passed on his contact's mobile number and asked us to contact him. We finalised the plan with him.

"By the way, where are you planning to get the papers xeroxed?" Chottu asked

"We've got a machine at Sahail's place," I replied

"That's wonderful. Best of luck. Let me know if you need any help."

This was going on at one end; on the other, I did my research on rental agreements, talked to friends' fathers who were lawyers, and learnt about the important things that had to be written into the agreement. The lawyers prepared the draft, but we revised it based on the inputs we got from relatives and friends. We went through at least five drafts before the final one was made.

Exams began. The first one was physics. The night before the exam, we got a call from the agent and went and picked up the papers. The guy came in a fancy SUV car and rolled down the window. "What are your names?" he asked.

"Aryan. And this is my friend, Sahail."

"Here, take the papers. Be careful. Do not get caught."

He rolled up the window and left.

We looked on in disbelief. Until the last minute, I was doubtful about getting the paper, but this was for real. Soon, copies were made. We dropped off the first copy at Arvind's room; then, we went around distributing the papers and collecting money from all the guys who wanted the physics paper. We came back to Arvind's room, Rs. 15,000 richer. The answer sheet was ready. We began to study. By 6a.m., I had mugged up the answers for the entire 50 marks. I asked Arvind for help with more. Sahail went to sleep saying, "Bhai, I just want to pass!"

At 9a.m., we were in the exam hall. Shivers ran down my spine when they began to distribute the papers. I got a copy in my hand. I quickly turned over to the first page and yelled, "Yes!"

"Shhhhh!" The teachers gave me a stern look. I turned around to see Sahail. He also looked happy. We both began to write the answers before we forgot what we had mugged up. Suddenly, a flying squad entered the examination hall. They were in charge of surprise checks. They came straight towards me – I guess smiling while writing the answers was a total giveaway. They searched me from top to bottom – my shoes and the inner lining of my clothes – but didn't find anything. I laughed to myself.

When the exam was over, we rushed back to the apartment. As soon as we entered, we both screamed and hugged each other. "Yes! We did it!" Our joy knew no bounds. The phone began to ring with requests for the next exam paper, which was maths. Even the guys who had refused the offer earlier asked for the remaining papers.

I told Sahail, "It looks like we stand to collect a cool 30,000 rupees on the next paper."

"Awesome! Good marks and money. This is turning out to be the best days of my life!"

"Where is the 15k?" I asked.

"Below the fish tank."

I took it and we went to Sankey Road – the same place that the guy had asked us to come to pick up the paper. He was in his car, smoking.

"Boss, here you go. Thanks a lot. When do we come for the math paper?" I asked.

"Same time. I will message you the place. How did it go? All well?" he asked.

"Everything went well. In fact it was awesome," we replied.

"Good. I will get in touch once the other paper is ready."

We collected the next paper from him and followed the same process of distribution, but this time the number of rounds were more, as we had more than twice the number of clients. By the time we got to the hostel to start studying, it was 7.30.

"Where were you guys? I tried calling you from Mohit's mobile," Arvind said.

"Why? Any problem?" Sahail asked.

"No...These are complicated questions. It will take time to mug..."

We got down to it and tried to study. I went through the examination and came out with a bad feeling that I hadn't written down all that I had mugged up. Sahail had the same feeling. Anyway, the 'feel good' factor was that we had made 15,000 rupees extra in last night's collection. We went and paid the agent. Someone else was driving the car this time; he did not introduce us to him. That person just looked at us through his sunglasses. We got more calls for the last paper. It looked like a haul of at least Rs. 45,000 extra.

We sat with Arvind and studied for the next four exams. In fact, I went through the entire textbook and all the notes. Sahail studied just enough to pass, and a little more. It felt really good walking out of those exams. I knew that at least 70 percent marks were coming my way without help from any agent or exam papers.

After the fourth exam, there was a break in between papers, so mom had set that date for finalising the agreement. All the involved parties signed the agreement. Dad was called in last. He came in, signed and walked back into his room. I saw less of dad in the days that followed. I told myself that once the exams were over, I would use the money I had earned by selling papers to buy something for dad. The agreement was done; from now on, we would receive Rs. 20,000 every month. Looked like chicken was back on the menu!

The final exam was electrical science – and it was the biggest order we had received. At 12a.m. sharp, we received a call to come to Castle Street in Sadashiv Nagar – a new location – to collect the papers. I knew the location; the only problem was that the street was a dead end. The previous two places were out in the open – one on an empty ground and the other near a lake. Why had the guy asked us to come to a dead end lane this time? Sahail rode towards Sadashiv Nagar. I asked him to stop at the crossroad. We called the guy and asked, "Where are you?"

"I'm in Castle Street. Where are you?"

I took the mobile from Sahail and spoke: "Our bike has some problem. We are at the crossroad, one lane before the location. Can you come here? Till then, we'll see what's happened to the bike."

"No...That's not the plan. You come here."

"Okay, but please wait for some time. We need to fix the bike...give us five minutes." I hung up.

"What's wrong with you Aryan? The bike is fine. What are you playing at?" Sahail asked.

"I don't have time to explain. Call Mohit and give me the phone," I replied.

"Hi Mohit, Aryan here. I need a favour from you. I am coming to your room to xerox some papers. Is that okay?"

"Aryan, I know what you are going to xerox. Sorry, but I can't allow you to cheat in front of my eyes, and right in my hostel room. Don't call me regarding this matter anymore."

"Mohit, wait! Don't hang up. I've got something, that I can offer you."

"I don't need the paper, Aryan. I can study and get good marks."

That was true – he was one of the rich geeks of our college, and a straightforward and upright guy.

"No Mohit, not the paper. I know about your crush on Anjali."

There was silence.

"I will see that Sahail breaks all contact with her. The rest of it is up to you." This was my offer at the time of need.

"Are you serious?" he asked.

"Yes!" I replied.

"Okay. Come over soon, before I change my mind."

Sahail was shocked, and looked at me as though I had snatched candy from a kid.

"Sahail, please, just follow my lead."

A car came up and the window was rolled down. Our agent was inside the car.

"What is taking you guys so long?" he asked from inside the car.

"Boss, the bike broke down. We have called our friend to bring another bike. He is on his way..."

"I don't have time for this. Here, take the paper and give me the money."

As per our deal, for the last paper, money had to be given upfront in exchange for the paper. Sahail was reaching in to get his wallet, when I said, "Boss! We have to collect it from our friends. I will give it to you tomorrow for sure – one hundred percent."

"You assholes! What do you think of yourselves? We had a deal. I am sorry, I can't give you the paper."

"Okay boss." I returned the paper and said, "I will go and collect the money and come back." He stared at me for a while, and then said, "Keep it. Pay me tomorrow without fail!" He rolled up his window and drove away. I jumped onto the bike, started it and shouted to Sahail to jump on fast. We sped away, but in a different direction – not towards college.

"Aryan, where are we going? What's happening?"

"Sahail, it's a trap. I will explain later. Right now, I need you to inform all the parties involved to meet at different locations, far away from the original location. Sahail, send only messages! Wipe out all call records and messages in drafts and inbox. Wipe out everything."

I reached the hostel; we went to Mohit's room and xeroxed the required number of copies. While I was making the copies, Mohit was staring at Sahail; I knew Sahail would react. I quickly said, "Sahail, go and get Arvind here. Fast."

Sahail left and came back with Arvind.

"Arvind, you are going to study in Mohit's room and sleep here tonight," I said while I was scribbling something on every sheet. Mohit objected, and Arvind said, "No, I will sleep in my room and study there."

"Listen to me you nerds! Do as I say or both of you will get a beating – and it'll be a serious one!" I was irritated.

They both became silent. Sahail helped Arvind shift his books to Mohit's room.

"Sahail, you stay here. I'll go and come back," I said

"No Aryan. I am coming with you. If you get caught, you will need company in jail. And, if I stay here, I will kill Mohit and land up alone in jail."

I laughed. We left to distribute the papers and collect the money. The last xerox copy was slid into a white car parked outside on the road. We collected Rs. 45,000.

It was 8a.m. We both knew that we were going to fail. We rushed back to hostel and studied what Arvind had prepared. There was some commotion in the corridor. I told everyone in the room to shut the windows and concentrate on the paper. We left the hostel at five minutes to 9. Before we left, I took all the answer sheets, rough papers and notebooks and stuffed them into the dustbin, along with the question paper, and burned it. Then, I put the ashes into a plastic bag and threw it into a dustbin on the way to college. While heading towards the examination hall, I said something to Mohit quietly. Sahail was very irritated with my secretive behaviour. Mohit picked up his phone and made a call.

Sahail asked me, "Who is he speaking to? Hope he is not getting us into trouble."

"Don't worry, I asked him to call someone on my behalf."

The exam began. Another squad came in. This time, they checked Sahail and me for chits. They were unsuccessful. I smirked at them as they left the room. The exam got over at 12. When we came out of the hall, we were arrested by the cops. On questioning them as to why they were arresting us, I received a slap on my cheek from the Sub Inspector.

"This is not America, where I have to tell you anything before you are arrested." said the Sub Inspector.

Sahail and I were taken to the jeep. Inside the jeep was the xerox machine from Sahail's house, along with Sahail's cook. The poor boy was weeping. I told him to relax, and said that it would all be okay soon. "Just shut your mouth," The Sub Inspector said, irritated with my arrogance. I was sure that it would all be okay. All that the cook could reveal to them was that we were xeroxing some papers – that was not a crime in India.

We reached the police station. The inspector began to question us.

"So, distributing the examination papers?"

"Sorry sir, we are not teachers to distribute papers," I replied.

"Shut up! This is a serious offense," he said.

"Yes sir. I know it's a serious offense, but what does it have to do with us?" I asked.

"Why do you need a xerox machine?"

"To xerox notes for our project, assignments..."

"You bloody fellow! Shut your mouth, I say! Is this not your machine? I am asking the fair boy!" said the Sub Inspector. From the way he spoke, I figured he had definitely passed his English exams by cheating.

"Answer me, I say!" It was like a scene from the movies. I found it hard to control my laughter.

"To xerox, sir."

"What, my dear?"

"Notes, sir," Sahail replied. I began to grin.

Whack! Sahail also got a slap.

There was some commotion outside the police station. Chottu was handcuffed and brought inside the station by a Senior Officer. The press was there, taking photos. He looked at us with blood-shot eyes.

"Hey, asshole! Did you think we are fools? Now, enjoy your term behind bars," I whispered in Chottu's ears while he stood next to us, as the Sub Inspector and Assistant Commissioner of Police (ACP) talked amongst themselves.

Sahail was shocked at what was happening. The ACP came up to us, apologised and asked the Sub Inspector to set us free. He explained to us that we had been wrongly accused. Chottu was put behind bars. I walked up to the Sub Inspector and told him. "Sir, it looks like you were up the whole night trying to capture the wrong person. You look very tired and need rest. We need to meet sometime soon." I rubbed my cheek as I spoke.

Outside the station, Mohit, Arvind and a few other friends had gathered and were waiting for us.

"Thanks yaar! You saved us!" I said as I hugged Mohit.

"Tell this guy not to fool around with Anjali anymore," Mohit joked to lighten the mood

"I will do that," I replied.

We went back to the apartment. I lit a cigarette.

Sahail asked, "What the heck is going on here? Can you please tell me?"

"Chottu was trying to set us both up for some jail time."

"What? But he was the one who gave us the agent's number!"

"That agent was an ex-cop, one of his dad's cronies."

"How did you know? If you knew, why did you go ahead with such a risky affair?"

"Hold on. I will explain everything in detail. The first paper was a trap. They didn't intend to catch us then, but they needed proof that we would get involved. We took the bait. Normally, in the first dealing, everyone is careful and on high alert. So, they didn't move in. If they did, there would only be charges of buying the exam paper and, under third degree treatment, we would have eventually mentioned Chottu's name and pulled him into the crime.

"For the second paper, they followed us and noted down all our drop points for the exchange of exam papers and money. Chottu was the one who gave the idea to sell the papers to other people, to make some money. Through this, they would be able to establish, that we were the main dealers who were distributing papers around Bangalore. Now, they knew our route, where we were copying the paper and people we were distributing the paper to. I am pretty sure they would have also taken pictures of us handing over papers to others. Luckily, we always put the examination paper between normal white sheets of paper, folded it and then handed it over to them. So if they arrested us at that time and the people testified that we sold the papers to them, we would have become the main distributors since no one else knew Chottu or the agent. It would be our word against theirs. Chottu had group studies at his home just to establish a firm alibi for himself. So, we would get stuck in this case as the main culprits.

"The day before the final paper, I was at Najji's bakery. I met a senior from Chottu's batch. He asked me about the exams. I told him that we were somehow managing and asked him about his exams. He told me it was a total mess – it was very difficult and that he was mostly going to fail the exams. I felt sorry for him and told him to ask Chottu for help.

'Arey bhai! Chottu doesn't help others. He wants to get first rank for himself. This time, I heard, he has arranged some sort of study group for all VIP fellows. Where can fellows like us fit into that group, bhai?'

'Who? Chottu?'

'Yes bhai. He is a merit seat holder.'

"That didn't make sense to me. Why would a merit seat holder require exam papers? I knew something was not right. Guys who get the paper leaked don't try to get first rank as it attracts too much attention. Anyway, I thought, why do I have to break my head over that? We were getting the original paper and making money off that. What else did I need? I came back to your apartment and began killing time on Orkut, when I stumbled upon Chottu's post – 'What goes around comes around'. I snooped around his profile and found his father's photo. I had seen this face somewhere else.

"I checked online about Prakash Gowda, his father's name. He was an ACP. I found in a newspaper report five years back, he was accused of selling engineering and medical exam papers, but was acquitted as the charges against him were false. This information got me wondering. So, Chottu's father was the one arranging the papers for us. Maybe he was embarrassed to tell us that his father was involved in such activities. Who wouldn't be?

"Still, I didn't have any doubt about this being a game against us, till we got ready to go and collect our papers.

"You kept getting calls from Anjali that night, but you didn't pick it up, knowing we were on our way to collect the paper. Finally you got a message from her, while we were waiting in the usual place for the agent – 'He has proposed'. Both of us thought it was Mohit, the rich lover boy who was interested in Anjali, but it was actually Chottu. As we were about to reach Castle Street, my intuition made me stop the bike a couple of lanes before. Things began to fall into place. It struck me like lightning – that psycho was trying to get both of us out of the way and strike a chord with Anjali and get his revenge. Somehow, I knew they would only catch us, when we began distributing the papers ourselves."

"Why didn't you pay him? We had the money," asked Sahail.

"Idiot! When you know that we are mostly going behind bars because of this idiot, why would I pay him? So I took a different route to college and asked you to message all the boys who were going to receive the paper to come to a different location. I called up your cook and asked him to burn all waste paper, xerox papers and every other loose paper there was and dispose off everything in the sink. I directed him to remove the ink cartridge and destroy it."

"When did you do all this?"

"When you went to get Arvind?" I replied.

"But the cops could have gotten hold of any of those guys we gave the paper to and extracted information from them."

"I wrote a note on every copy except one: 'Write down the questions in a haphazard manner in different books and burn the paper-police on trail.'"

Sahail was looking at me in astonishment. "What about the one paper you didn't write a note on?"

"That was the paper I slid into the boot of the white Hyundai."

"Whose car was it?"

"Prakash Gowda's car. Chottu's father's car."

"Why his father's car?"

"Gowda, who opened the rear boot space of his car to oblige for the search, noticed the examination paper there. To escape from the law, he had to blame his son. This time, there was evidence, and it would have been difficult to get out on bail. So, the son became the scapegoat for the father."

"Bloody hell! You made a father accuse his own son!"

"I wanted the asshole to know how it feels to be betrayed by someone you trust."

"How did the cops find him?"

"While you were studying, I checked the net for the old case involving his father and which cop handled the case. I found the details of the cop who had handled that case. He is now an ACP in the crime branch." I paused for a minute to light up another cigarette. "It was the same guy who got us out and put Chottu behind bars. It was a matter of prestige for him, as he was dishonoured and suspended for filing a fake FIR against Prakash's father five years back."

"How did you contact him?"

"I didn't. I gave all the details to Mohit before the exam. Mohit made the call that you were concerned about. I also told him to call the press after the exam and ask them to come to Mathikere station, because the mastermind behind the engineering paper leak was going to get arrested soon. The rest you know."

"What an ass of a fellow, that Chottu!"

"He was waiting for an opportunity to get back at us, and be able to propose to Anjali."

"But his father will get him out soon," Sahail said

"Still, he has lost his name, his money and, most importantly, his respect," I said while I poured out a drink for myself. "He won't bug us anymore. Anyway, how much did we make?"

"Bhai, 15,000 from the second paper and 45,000 from the third."

"Sahail, it was 60,000 from the third. We don't have to pay that agent!"

"Oh yes...wow! A cool 75,000.We must celebrate!"

"Okay, give me 2,000 bucks. I will go and buy meat and some drinks. You start the preparations. I have called Mohit and Arvind to join us for the evening."

"But Aryan, I hate that fellow...Mohit."

"That 'fellow' is one of the reasons you are out here, puffing a cigarette. Show him the respect he deserves."

I slammed the door behind me.

5. Love Blossoms

I started the bike and left. As I was going down the road through college, I saw Sanjanna standing on the other side in front of her hostel. I took a U-turn and went up to her.

"Hi, how was your exam?" I asked her.

"Oh, it was fine. Electrical science was quite tough," she replied

In the first semester of engineering, all subjects were common to all branches. I wondered if I should have given her the question paper – but would she have approved?

"Hello! What happened? What you dreaming about?"

"About the electrical science paper," I replied.

She began to giggle. She looked so pretty!

"Do you want to get some coffee?" I blurted out.

"Actually, I am waiting for my friends to pick me up. We are planning to go to 'The Club' later in the evening. Now, I am going to a friend's house, and then I will leave from his house."

My heart sank at my very first rejection. I could not take it.

"Come, sit on the bike. We will have coffee and I will drop you later to your friend's house." I spoke in a firm voice, hoping she would succumb.

She quietly sat on the bike. I didn't know if it was out of fear or if she actually liked the idea. I started the bike and left.

"Are you drunk?" she asked.

"No.Just had a beer to celebrate the completion of our exams."

"You smoke too?"

"Yes."

"How many cigarettes do you smoke a day?"

What was wrong with this girl? Why was she grilling me like my mom?

"Why? Are you planning on keeping track?" I asked.

We didn't talk till we reached the coffee shop. She ordered a tropical iceberg; I got an espresso.

"So, where are you from? Where is your hometown?" I asked. These two simple questions got an answer that was 30-minutes long. By the end of our coffee, I knew her mother's and father's favourite colours, the ice creams they liked and a bunch of unwanted, useless information about her uncles and aunts. Thank God, her mobile rang.

"Yes, yes, I am on the way...I am at Coffee Day...with Aryan...yup, the same one." Then she hung up the phone. I knew some bad comment had been made on the other side of that call.

"Who was it?" I asked.

"That was Rachana, my friend. All of them have reached Nikhil's place. We will be staying there for the night."

"You are going to be staying at an unknown guy's place?"

"Rachana is going to be there and couple of other girls too." She didn't have to justify her decision to me, but she did.

I dropped her off at Nikhil's place. Her friends were peering through the balcony. No one came down to say 'hi'. I left and went back to Sahail's place and rang the doorbell; Sahail opened the door and punched me in my stomach.

"What did you do that for, ass?" I asked as I doubled up in pain.

"We all were shit worried about you! Mohit went to the station to look for you, and I was roaming the entire college to see where you were. Why don't you keep a mobile like every normal person?"

"Sorry, I forgot. I met Sanjanna in front of the hostel."

The mood immediately shifted from irritation and anger to curiosity.

"What happened?" Sahail asked.

"I took her out for coffee."

Reactions ranged from "Oooh" to "Who? Sanjanna from computer science?" and "But how did you manage?"

"I asked her to sit on the bike and she did."

"Did you kidnap her, or did she come willingly?" Sahail asked, giggling.

"So, what next?" Mohit asked.

"I dropped her at her friend's place; they going to 'The Club' for a party."

"Come, let's go!" the rest shouted.

"Are you fellows mad? That is not our type of place; let's all enjoy here. Plus, I am not dressed for a club. If I go home now, drunk, to change, I will be whacked by my dad."

The truth was that I was broke and could not afford party clothes. Sahail knew this. "You don't have to go home to get your clothes – we can buy some on the way. Bhai, we have the money!"

Although I tried giving excuses for not going, deep down, I really did want to go. We rode up to a shopping mall first. I was looking at some shirts and pants, when Sahail pulled me into a leather goods shop and showed me a black leather jacket. I fell in love with it immediately. I got leather boots to go with it. I looked like an Italian gangster from the movies. Sahail also brought me a Nokia 3210; "Keep this with you. You have this dirty habit of disappearing suddenly; at least now we can find out where you are," he said.

The Club was in the outskirts of the city, and the parties went on till early in the morning. The only problem was that we were all guys. So, I needed a girl to enter the club to meet the girl I was interested in. We decided to sort out the problem once we reached the place. There was a commotion at the entrance. Ayub Khan, the Bollywood superstar, had come with his friends. I walked up to the crowd around him. He wore a tight black tee shirt and jeans, leather boots and a sliver bracelet. He was talking to the bouncer.

"Sir, you will have to pay entrance fees," said the bouncer.

"Do you know who I am?" replied Ayub Khan.

"Sir, you will still have to pay the entrance fees," the dumb bouncer said.

Ayub Khan took out a wad of notes and flung it at the bouncer. "Keep the change," he said and walked in with his hand around the waist of a girl he had come with. Soon, all his friends followed him. I sneaked into the group and went inside. I went back outside five minutes later; Sahail and the others were trying to buy their way in, but the bouncer was not letting them inside.

"Manager," I called out, and pointed to the boys. "They are with me. I came in with Ayub Khan." The manager allowed them inside, but followed us. I hugged Sahail and told the gang to follow my lead. We went down to Ayub Khan's table. The manager observed us from a distance. He knew he already pushed his luck with his bouncer asking Ayub Khan to pay; he was not going to cross the line again.

"Hello sir. I saw what they did to you at the entrance. My friends and I have protested to the manager," I said to Ayub Khan and pointed to the manager. "What he did was wrong! How dare he stop a superstar like you?"

Ayub khan stood up and hugged me. "See, this fellow knows the value of a star!" He turned around and shouted, "You bloody manager, come here!"

The manager, who was standing at a distance, didn't hear a word because of the loud music. Ayub Khan gestured for him to come closer, and the Manager ran over to his table.

"These boys are with me. Take care of them like you would take care of me. I paid your entrance fees and will pay your bill, but if you misbehave with them, you will lose your job for sure," Ayub Khan said in a loud voice. He meant business.

"No sir, I will give them my utmost interest and service. Sorry for the entrance fees. The drinks and food are on the house." Ayub Khan patted my cheek and told me to "Enjoy!"

Sahail looked at me. "Bloody! An acting award should be given to you!"

"No, a fraud award should be given to him!" Mohit butted in. This was Mohit's problem – he didn't know when he should keep quiet. I ignored him and asked Arvind to wait at the entrance and inform whenever Sanjanna came.

The manager came to us every five minutes to ask if everything was all right. Soon, Arvind came running to our table. "Bhai, she has come but the bouncer is not allowing her friend's and her as club is full."

I went outside and met Sanjanna. She was shocked.

"What are you doing here?" she asked.

"Why? Am I not allowed here?" I replied.

"No, no...Was just wondering. I am surprised to see you here. Have you come alone?" She was wondering if I had come with some girl.

"No. Came with some friends."

"Who? Sahail?" She needed a confirmation from my side that there was no girl waiting for me inside.

"Yeah, and some other friends too."

"It looks like we can't get in because the club is full."

"Wait for a minute; I will sort things out."

I went in and spoke to the manager. He went outside and invited Sanjanna and her friends to come inside. I was at the lobby, waiting for them.

"Anything else, sir?" the Manager asked me.

"Nothing, chief. Thanks a lot."

"Sir, it's my duty. After all, you are Ayub Khan's guest."

Sanjanna and her friends were clearly shocked. They began to whisper among themselves.

Sanjanna took me aside and asked, "You know Ayub Khan?"

"Yeah, why?" My mind was telling me to go with the flow.

"You don't look like someone who goes out much."

"I choose not to party, but I have been coming here since 10th standard."

Lies! Lies! Lies! I was secretly hoping she would not ask me to take her around the place.

"Sanjanna, come. We are leaving," Nikhil, one of her friends, shouted to her.

"Why? We just got here," Sanjanna replied as she walked towards her friends.

I was irritated. By then, Sahail, Mohit and Arvind had come to the Lobby. Sanjanna and her friends were talking amongst themselves; we could not hear what they were saying because of the loud music in the background. After some time, Sanjanna came up to me and said, "We are leaving. The place is too packed for our comfort."

Sahail chipped in, "We have our own table. You can..."

"Okay Sanjanna. See you. Bye," I bluntly cut off Sahail's comment. She walked away.

Sahail turned to me. "Why did you do that?"

"If she only listens to her friends and does not have a mind of her own, they will always be able to influence her. I don't want to be with someone whose mind is influenced by another person."

"Break-up, before he could even propose," Mohit said.

The next minute, Mohit was on the ground with his hand to his mouth – it was bleeding because I had punched him.

"Learn what to say, and when to say it," I told him.

Sahail began to laugh; he helped Mohit up and led him to the loo. When they came back to the table, Mohit's lips were swollen.

"Sit down and have a drink, you will feel better," I told him.

"No, seeing that girl....ahhhh... ditch...you...made me feel good," Mohit was trying to laugh, but he was in pain.

"Ass, you will never change. Sit down, have a drink," I told him.

We began chatting, but I was distracted by other thoughts. *Who does that Nikhil think he is? Why is she listening to him? Forget it, Aryan – she is never going to be with a person like you. She is way out of your league. It is better to forget about her and move on with your life.*

"So, bhai, will you clear all papers?" Sahail asked me.

"No, I will tug in maths and electrical."

"What? I gave you the answer sheet to mug," Arvind said.

"I could not mug; there was no time."

Mohit laughed. "So, you guys going to fail despite getting hold of the papers. You fellows must be the dumbest guys on the planet."

"We made Rs. 75,000. We are not dumb; we just chose money over education," I said.

"Money is not everything," Mohit said.

"That from a guy who has a Xerox machine in his room," I teased.

"You will do anything for money?" Mohit asked me.

"Try me," I replied.

There was silence. We drank for some time and decided to leave. As we were leaving, Ayub Khan came up to me. He reeked of alcohol and smoke. "I heard you punched this guy," he said, pointing at Mohit.

"Yes."

"Whaa!" He put his hands around my shoulder. "Remember this: kings are not always kings. It is only a period in your life. Treasure those close to you." He was drunk.

"Okay boss, thanks."

"Goodnight." We hugged him like we were good friends. I went back to Sahail's room and collapsed on the bed. It had been a hectic three weeks.

The next day, I was woken up by Sahail's screams: "Fuck! Fucking shit!"

"What happened? Why you screaming?" I asked him.

"Come, see for yourself!"

"What is it?" I asked as I began to sip water slowly from a bottle. I had a splitting headache from last night's drinking session.

"They are going to have a re-examination because of the paper leak!"

I spat the water out and grabbed the paper. The front-page headlines read as follows:

"VTU first semester papers have been leaked. Accused Pratap Gowda is behind bars. It is not clear if all papers where leaked, but it has been confirmed that the electrical science paper was leaked. The VTU chancellor has announced that there will be re-examination for the confirmed paper that has been leaked. The re-examination will take place after two days. A probe into the matter is being continued by the Crime Branch."

I collapsed onto the sofa. I guess I was happy that I had another chance to write the exam. My thoughts went to the people and the money they paid us. Soon, we were bombarded by calls. I explained to them that we had given them the original paper. Now, the University had decided to hold a re-exam, which was not our fault. The next question was whether we could arrange for the new exam papers – my answer was 'No'.

Sahail began studying; I opened the book and realised that it was not possible to study in two days. I decided to skip the exam. The next day, a detailed article talked about how they had captured the kingpin in the paper racquet scam; he was involved in previous cases too. It also described how many students across the state had had to cancel their tickets back home. The mass cancellations and re-booking of tickets were causing loss to the students and gains to the travel agencies. My little adventure had truly affected every single engineering student of that year.

On the day of the exam, I stayed at home. My parents were unaware of the developments. My father didn't read the paper, and my mother was too busy handling family issues. Sahail called me once it was over.

"Bhai, come, let's get a drink. I am failing the paper for sure. People were saying it was the toughest paper ever set."

"Okay. I will come over in the evening."

When I reached his apartment, I saw Arvind and Mohit there, drowning their sorrows.

"Come Sahail, let's go get some more drinks," I said.

"No bhai, you get it for us. We have been drinking from lunchtime. I can't even stand straight."

"Okay. Where is the money?" I had left all the money with Sahail.

"In the suitcase behind the counter"

On the way to get the drinks, while passing the college, I spotted Sanjanna with her friends.

I turned away and ignored her even though she waved at me. I pretended that I had not seen her.

Later that evening, I got a message from an unknown number: 'Mister, why are you acting rude and ignoring me?'

'Who is this?' I replied.

'Sanjanna here.' She texted back

'Hi Sanjanna. When did I ignore you? How did you get my number?' I sent her a message

'Don't lie. You saw me today, but you just rode off.'she texted back

'No, I didn't see you.' I was lying; I had seen her. She was wearing a beautiful blue salwar-kameez.

'Can you come meet me now?'

'I am having drinks with my friends.'

'Come for 5 minutes. Anyway, have to get back inside the hostel by 10.30.'

Why did she want to meet me? 'Okay. Come down in five minutes.'

I got up to leave. "Where are you off too?" Sahail asked.

"I am coming in five minutes."

"You never come in five minutes. Who are you going to meet?"

I just walked out and started the bike. She was waiting for me outside the hostel; she was dressed in a loose tee shirt and jeans. When I parked the bike, she sat behind me and said, "Let's go to the night canteen." She wrapped her hands around my waist and hugged me. Shivers ran up my spine. I rode slowly as I was enjoying every moment. When we reached our destination (in two minutes), I parked the bike and we both got off.

"What was that?" I asked her.

"Nothing. It was cold," she replied.

"So, you hug anyone if it's cold?"

"No. I felt like hugging you, so I hugged."

I was confused. Was she hugging me like a friend? Or, did she like me?

"Okay. What did you want to see me for?" I asked her.

"What were you drinking?"

"Bacardi with Coke."

"Are you celebrating the completion of the exams?"

"I didn't write the last one."

"Why?"

"I didn't want to study it again."

"Okay. Come, drop me back."

"You called me out to ask what was I drinking?"

"No, you idiot. I wanted to see you."

"Why?"

"Because...I think I like you."

"You think you like me?"

"Yeah, I missed talking to you." She acted as if we had been speaking for years, but I decided to go along with her version.

"At The Club, you only wanted to be with your friends."

"You didn't let me finish. My friends wanted to leave; I was ready to stay back if you could put me up in some place till morning. I came to ask you that, but you cut me off so rudely in front of your friends."

"Oh..."

"What 'oh'? Do you like me?"

"Yes."

She came and hugged me tightly. We hugged for a while before she said, "Control yourself, you horny fellow! Take me back."

We rode back. This time, she hugged me tightly. It felt really good. I dropped her off, picked up some more liquor and went back to Sahail's place. They were preparing chicken curry. I announced, "Sanjanna and I are seeing each other!"

"What?" they chorused.

I told them what had happened. Sahail laughed and shouted, "The geek and the rowdy – what a love story this is going to turn out to be!"

Little did he realise this was going to change me – and make me what I have become today.

6. The Problems Begin

The results were announced. As predicted, I had failed in mathematics and electrical science. Sanjanna called me from her hometown and asked me to check her results; back then, the results were pinned up on the board and not posted on the Internet. After seeing her results, I felt worse – the geek had passed with a total aggregate of 83 percent.

I called her to tell her the results; she was very happy.

"What about you, Aryan?"

"I tugged in two subjects."Even though I got the the question paper

"Which ones?"

"Mathematics and Electrical science."

"Oh...poor baby. When I come back, I will help you out."

I felt the knife slip in deeper. "No need. I will manage," I replied.

"Oh, you male chauvinist pig! A girl can't help you or what?"

"A girl can. You can't."

"You pig! Wait till I get back – I will spank you!"

"Come back soon – now, even I am waiting for my spanking!"

"You horny guy – Is that all you can think off?! Anyway, chat with you later."

During this time, Dev grew up to be a notorious fellow. He would get into petty fights, but get away from trouble because he was my younger brother – people who knew me would help settle the issues. Soon, he started to stay away from home. Drinking, partying and fighting became his main source of entertainment. Every time he did something stupid, mom would call me and I would have to go after him to bring him back or get him out of trouble.

Whenever I spent time with Sanjanna, I would get a call saying that Dev had ran away from home or that he had gotten into a fight. So, I would drop her back at the hostel and head home. One day, she asked me, "Why do you go to help him out every time?"

"Sanjanna, he is family."

"I also believe in family, but you are going over the top to help your brother. If he is old enough to drink, he is old enough to handle his problems. I don't see him coming to help you out."

"Every man lives by a code – my code is family. Whether he is wrong or right, it is my duty as the elder brother to protect him."

"You are spoiling him. One day, you will realise that."

I did not reply to that statement. I dropped her at the hostel, then picked up Sahail and left for my house. He was aware of all that Dev was up to. Mom told me, "Dev had an argument with me and ran away from home again."

"Where has he gone this time? Any idea?" I asked

"No idea. He came home, we had a fight, and he left"

I did not want to know what the fight was about. I began to make a few calls to his friends and found out where he was holed up.

I told mom, "I will go get him."

"Whose house has he gone to?" mom asked.

"He is at DJ Ajay's place." He was Dev's classmate, but had dropped out of school to pursue his career as a disc jockey. Sahail and I went to Ajay's place. His grandfather opened the door.

"Is Dev here?"

"Yes, just a minute...Dev, some people to see you."

Dev and Ajay walked out from his room. Dev saw me and looked down. When he came closer to us, I told him to go down and wait for us.

After Dev went down, Sahail went close to Ajay and said, "The next time we find that fellow here, I won't be speaking to you so politely."

Ajay looked at me and said, "Aryan, I didn't want him to sleep on the pavement, so I gave him shelter."

"If he comes here for shelter, ask him to leave. Once he sleeps on the footpath, he will get straightened out," I replied.

We took Dev home. After some drama at home, Dev and mom went to sleep. Sahail and I went to the terrace for a smoke. Sahail knew about my father's situation and I knew about his. He couldn't disagree or talk back to his father, even when he wanted something else. His father was a powerful man in Jammu, and his son was like a mouse in front of him. Both our families were quite messed up.

Soon, the second semester was upon us. This time, we decided to study to get through the examination. We also had the option of clearing our back subjects. I began to study hard. Sanjanna called me on my landline a few times. Mom was not too pleased. "Why is that girl calling you during exam time? She is trying to distract you. These days, girls are overtaking boys by using such tactics."

How could I explain to mom that I was no innocent guy, and that Sanjanna was a rank student? I chose to ignore her complaints. This time, I passed all my subjects and cleared one of my back papers with 66 percent. I called mom to tell her the results. She merely said, "That's all? If you got another four percent you would have gotten a distinction. Work harder next time."

I was angry with mom. She didn't encourage me, and didn't express any sort of happiness. At least Sanjanna was happy – she hugged me in front of everyone in college and shouted, "Congrats! Awesome!"

I felt happy. I told her what mom had told me. "Your mom expects too much from you," she said. I did not know if that was a statement of support or if she was trying to tell me that I was incapable of scoring more marks.My thoughts were broken as I heard Sahail crying; he failed in most of the subjects, and had to repeat another year. He called his mother and informed her. After a while, he got a call from his father.

"Re- attempt."

"NO."

"Please let me continue in civil."

"Okay"

"Okay"

"Okay"

These were his answers. After he hung up the phone, I asked him what had happened.

"Dad wants me to shift to medical electronics. Supposedly there is huge scope in Jammu for this branch."

"Are you planning to join medical electronics?" I asked him.

"I don't want to, but I can't refuse my father's decision."

It was set – from the next year, we were all going to be in separate branches. Sahail planned to go home for the vacation to see if he could convince his father about continuing in civil engineering. He handed over the keys of his apartment to me.

"Sanjanna, I got Sahail's apartment keys."

"So? Why are you telling me this?"

"Come back couple of days before vacation gets over."

"Why?"

"We can spend some alone time in Sahail apartment."

"Aryan, I am not that type of girl! What do you think of me?"

I silently cursed myself for asking her so directly. "No, sorry, I didn't mean it like that..." I began to stammer.

"Anyway, I will see you two days before vacations get over at the usual bus stop. Pick me up and we can go to Sahail's place," she giggled.

I picked her up and took her to Sahail's place. The moment we got inside and locked the door, she pounced on me and we began kissing and undressing each other.

I lifted her up and she wrapped her legs around me as I carried her to the bed. I threw her onto the bed and took out a box of condoms. "Our target is to finish this box," I said. She smiled.

We went through the whole box of honeymoon pack condoms. We drank, ate, watched TV and made love for the next two days. After two days, I dropped her back at her hostel. Sahail came back depressed; his father didn't agree to his proposition. He was to switch to medical electronics. He saw the cover of the honeymoon pack.

"Sanjanna came here?" he asked.

"Yeah," I replied.

"It was about time," he said.

7. Addiction

It was third semester in civil engineering. It felt like it had taken me a lifetime to get there. Once the classes began, it was really interesting. I made new friends, but met Sahail in the evenings. Sahail also made new friends in his batch; most of them were into drugs and were on a perpetual high.

"Sahail, don't you think it's better to stay away from those guys?" I asked him.

"And hang around with whom? You managed to get through. I am stuck here and am going to be here for a few more years than required, I am sure." Tears welled up in his eyes.

"Sahail, you will get through. It is matter of just four years."

"You think I will get through this in four years? I hate everything about medical electronics. It's not enough I have to study the human body – I have to study electronics as well. It is like trying to be half-doctor, half-engineer. I can't even understand a word they speaking in college. I am stuck here Aryan. I am going to be here for a long time!"

"How are the girls in your class?" I tried to change the topic.

"There is this one girl, Pooja...I mean, she is like WOW!" Sahail replied with a gleam in his eyes.

"No wonder you can't understand anything in class!" We both laughed. "What about Anjali?"

"She is still with me."

"Mohit?"

"I took Anjali to Mohit; we all sat down and talked. Anjali explained to Mohit how much she loves me and that we are meant to be together," Sahail replied.

"Mohit agreed?"

"What agreed? I made Anjali tie a rakhi on Mohit's hand. Now, he is her rakhi brother."

"Poor Mohit. You don't love Anjali – then why are you playing with her life?"

"She is mine."

"It's just for your ego, you useless fellow. What about Pooja?"

"Once she in the bag, I will break up with Anjali."

"One day, all of these girls will join together and hire some goons to beat the crap out of you!"

"Why do you think I made friends with you?" Sahail replied. I jokingly flung the glass at him.

With time, I saw less of Sahail as he spent more time in the hostel with his new friends. One day, I got a call from his cook. He told me that Sahail had not come back home for four days. I told him I would go check out the hostel.

On the way to the hostel, I met Ghoush Khan, one of my batch mates. He asked me, "Where to, bhai?"

"To the commerce hostel. Sahail has not come back to the apartment for a couple of days."

"You want me to come along?" Ghoush Khan asked.

"Okay, come."

We went around the hostel looking for Sahail. In the third floor, an entire corridor was known as the 'ganja corridor'. All the drug addicts had taken rooms close to each other. No one went in there without the aim of getting high. They were a violent bunch of fellows and people stayed far away from them.

For example, there was this guy called Raghuveer who went for a movie at the local theatre. During the break, he walked up to the food counter and ordered a packet of chips and a Coke. Some others objected as they were standing in a queue and he had cut in. Soon, a scuffle broke out between him and four local guys. He beat them up so badly, they begin to flee the scene. To add salt to their humiliation, Raghuveer caught one of the fellows and bit his nose off! He freaking bit his nose off – and spat it out on the floor! After that, he went outside, washed his mouth and lit a smoke, and stood outside the theater as though nothing had happened. Soon, the cops arrested him and a case was filed. His father's lawyers got him out on bail.

Raghuveer was just one of the 30 or 40 boys staying in the corridor. This corridor was so famous in our college that no one ventured to the third floor of the commerce hostel even by mistake. Even the security guards and wardens stayed away from that area as much as possible.

Ghoush and I entered that corridor. Some fellows were sitting in the corridor, smoking and playing a guitar. One of them recognised me. "Bhai, what brings you here today?" He was a short Nepali guy called Praveen.

"Where is Sahail?" I asked.

"He is in my room. Come."

We entered the room and were taken aback. Sahail lay on the floor; he had passed out. The room was filled with the smell of ganja. They had made a special bong to smoke weed. The normal yellow bulb light was replaced with a dim red light. The walls had been spray painted with images of dragons and gargoyles. Pieces of aluminum foil were scattered all over the room.

"Do you want to smoke one of these?" Praveen asked, waving a joint in the air.

"No. I just came to take Sahail."

"Let him rest. Once he gets up, he will come back on his own," replied Praveen

"Praveen, I am not asking you. I am telling you that I am taking him back."

"Bhai, I am also telling you not to use force here. Sahail came here on his own, and he will go back on his own. Why are you interfering in his life?"

Ghoush looked at me and then charged at Praveen and began raining blows at him. Praveen began to scream. I picked up Sahail, put his arm around my shoulder and dragged him out. Upon listening to Praveen's screams, the entire corridor came alive. It was as if we stirred a hornet's nest – many of them came rushing outside. I told Ghoush, "Enough. Come, let's go."

We started to walk down the corridor. Praveen's friends blocked our path. Raghuveer came up to me and asked, "Why you creating problems here?"

"No problem. I came to take my friend back."

At that time Praveen came out, blood dripping from his nose. "This fellow, Raghu, this fucking fellow..." he pointed at Ghoush. Raghu's hand went towards Ghoush; I caught it and pushed it away. We stared at each other.

After a while, he said, "Take your friend and leave. Never come back here again. If you do, we won't be responsible for the harm that befalls you or your friends."

Praveen butted in, "Raghu, how can we let them leave? I..." Raghu raised his hand and Praveen fell silent.

"I am letting you go, even though you have broken our friend's nose, because, when I was at this stage of my life, none of my friends or family came to help me. This world of drugs became my world. We are like the outcasts of society and we like it that way. It's a nice change to see someone who wants to help out people like us. We know this world is fucked up, but this is our world. The next time your friend comes here, he will not leave us – that for sure. Now take him and get lost."

I looked at the boys gathered there in the corridor. Their teeth were stained. Skin so pale, as if the life had been sucked out of them. Most of them had sunglasses on. Bodies covered with tattoos. Skinny fingers stained with tobacco.

Sahail was half-awake. We took him home. About four hours later, he got up, washed his face and lit a smoke.

"Sahail, what's happening here?" I asked.

"Who is this?" he pointed at Ghoush.

"My batch mate. He helped me get you out from that hell-hole."

"Why did you get me out from there? I was happy there. They are my family. I feel comfortable with them."

"Have you begun doing drugs?" I asked Sahail

"Yes."

"Why?"

"I felt like it! Why are you asking me all these questions? Stop irritating me."

Soon he was twitching and scratching his hair. I knew that this was not due to ganja alone – he had to have taken something else as well.

"What did you take, Sahail?"

"Heroin."

I was shocked. How did he fall into this crap? Questions aside, it was time to get him clean. I called up my home and told my mother I would be staying with Sahail for two weeks. I asked Ghoush to pick up some of my clothes from my place. I told him to buy a lock and some rope as well.

By evening, Sahail began to get restless. He got up, took his bike key and went towards the door. I asked him, "Where are you going?" He noticed that I had locked the main door from inside.

"Give me the key, bhai."

"Where are you going? Tell me."

"Just give me the damn key!"

"No."

"What do you mean by 'no'? This is my house! Who the fuck are you to say 'no'?" He went over and slapped his cook out of frustration. I asked Zabi to go inside the kitchen and lock it from inside. I got up from bed and walked up to Sahail. "You want hit somebody, hit me. Don't beat that small fellow to show your frustration," I said

"Just give me the keys. I need to go urgently. I promise I will come back soon."

"No," I replied sternly and turned away from him. He jumped on my back. I caught his hand and flung him onto the mattress and pressed my ankle on his chest. I grabbed the bed sheet close to me and tied both his hands tightly.

"Zabi, get that rope...quick!"

He came running with the rope. On seeing this, Sahail asked me, "What are you doing?" He was trying to wriggle his way out.

"Sahail, stay still or you will get hurt."

I tried to tie his legs down, but he began to scream, "Murder! Murder! Help! Help!"

He kept kicking his legs in the air. I caught one, placed my knee over his thigh and tied one end of the rope to that leg, then caught the other one and tied them together. I took the remaining length of rope and tied his hands to the top of the bedpost.

"Why are you doing this to me? Please let me go! My body is in pain! I promise I will stop!"

His screams continued for another other hour. The neighbours began to inquire. I spoke to them about the situation, and they were all very understanding, except for the apartment owner. After some time, Sahail gave up screaming. He was sweating profusely. I asked Zabi to pat his forehead with a cloth soaked with cold water. After that, I lit a cigarette and placed it in his mouth. He began to puff on it and then became calm. Every few hours, he would scream and complain of leg cramps and pain across his body. I would pat his forehead and give him a shot of rum and a smoke to calm him down. The next morning, he had to go to the loo. I locked the door and untied him. The moment I did that, he pounced on me and began to bite me. I punched him on the face, jumped on him and bit him on his shoulder. My teeth sank deep into his flesh and he began to bleed. I got off him; he sat up and began to laugh. "Bhai, I am truly blessed to have a friend like you!" He went into the loo; I washed my mouth at the kitchen sink. He came out after having a bath, walked up to me and said, "Tie me up. I don't know what I am capable of doing next."

Sanjanna called again and again. I didn't answer her calls. Then she sent a message: 'Where are you? Why are you not picking up? Spoilt me, now ignoring me huh?' She added a smiley face at the end. 'Will explain later...and you spoilt me!' I messaged back.

I tied Sahail up and switched on the TV. I told Zabi to clear the room of all sharp objects and to put them in the kitchen, which was to be locked at all times. Ghoush came to the house after college. He saw Sahail sweating and shivering, with froth coming out of his mouth.

"Bhai, I think you should take him to a hospital."

"And tell them what? The first thing they would do is to inform his parents. I know Sahail – if he knows his parents are aware of his drug problem, he will try something stupid."

The screams and groans of pain continued for a few days. We got him a hot water bag and placed it on his legs. In the evenings, I gave him a couple of pegs of rum to ease his nerves. Sanjanna was desperately trying to meet me, but I explained that Sahail needed my presence. As the days passed, he began to calm down. I locked him up, went to college and returned in the afternoon. We went out for walks. Soon, the cravings began to die down. He started to go to college. He had a cough and fever due to withdrawal symptoms. He kept away from his old friend group but we saw them on and off at the bakery. He would just nod at them, and they would acknowledge him. Anjali began to come to his apartment to take care of him. In fact, to prevent him from going back to drugs, she literally moved in with him. It was irritating for me, as we could not drink in peace thanks to her constant nagging (it was as if he was already married to her), but I was happy that she was there to look after him.

The following week, I met Sanjanna at the canteen. She looked depressed.

"Hi honey! Why are you looking so sad?" I asked her.

"Aryan, who do you think I am? You just disappeared – no calls, no communication. Did you even receive any of my calls?"

"Sweetie, you are aware of the situation. He needed me."

"Your brother needs you, your friends need you, but I don't need you?"

"Sweetie, I am truly sorry. Please forgive me." I removed a bunch of flowers from within my jacket.

She smiled and said, "This does not discount what you did."

"Yeah, I know." I caught her by the waist and pulled her close to me.

"Let go, you brute! People are watching."

"Let them watch."

"You have no problem. Anyway, the whole college thinks of you as a goonda."

"You are dating this goonda, my dear," I smiled.

"Yeah, I guess I am a sucker."

We made up and went for a movie. Later, I dropped her at the hostel and went back home.

8. Land Mafia

Mom was awake, waiting for me. "Aryan, we need to think of selling the factory land. The expenses have begun to grow and leaving the land empty like that is going to attract unwanted people."

"Okay, if you think that is best for the family, let's do it. What does dad say about this?'

"He is okay too."

That means Mom had arm-twisted him into agreeing. The word was put out and buyers turned up. Lots of people gave us a token advance of Rs. 1,001, but didn't come back or collect their advance. We must have collected at least Rs. 15,015 in token advances. What got me laughing was they gave an advance of Rs. 1,001 for land worth four crores. Soon, our lawyer got a builder who was interested – a young chap named Joseph Chetty. He agreed to the rate based on the validity of the papers. Soon, the process of handover of duplicate copies and talking to the lawyer began. My time after college was spent between the lawyer's place and Joseph's office. Dev was kept away from all this so that he could concentrate on his studies. Once the money came in, we could send Dev aboard for further studies. Soon, the agreement was signed by both parties. Dad was losing the final holding of his business.

A week later, I got a call from the guy who owned a telephone booth next to our factory. He informed me that some people had broken down our compound wall. I called up Joseph and asked him if it was his people. His reply was negative. I decided to go see it for myself. I took our old Maruti car and left for the factory. Indeed, the wall was broken down completely. I asked the labourers there as to why they had broken the compound wall. They replied, "Speak to our boss. He told us to break it."

"Who is your boss? Give me his number."

"Mr. Tony." They gave me a card

I called the number on the card.

"Hello."

"Mr. Tony, it seems you have instructed your labourers to break my compound wall."

"Who is this?"

"I am Aryan, Mr. Dutt's son."

"Aryan, the person we brought the land from told us that a part of your land belonged to him, so we broke the compound wall."

"Are you crazy? Some idiot tells you something, and, without asking anyone, you break down the compound wall!"

"Aryan, mind your language. Who do you think you are talking to? Go do whatever you can. Don't call me again." He hung up the phone.

I called mom and told her everything. "Why did you shout at him? There must be some misunderstanding... Fix a meeting with him. Let's all meet and resolve this amicably," she said.

If he wanted to resolve this, wouldn't he have approached us first? I wondered. Anyway, I called him and asked him if we could meet. He told us to come to his house at noon.

Mom and Dev came to his house; I was waiting for them. Dad did not come. His wife opened the door and let us in. We waited for him in his living room. After 15 minutes, he came down.

"Mrs. Dutt, sorry for the confusion. We brought the land to build an NGO for the elderly, so there is no monetary gain for us, and we are not land mafia to grab your land," he laughed. I was seething with anger.

"You could have informed us before demolishing the wall," said mom.

"Sorry madam, the people we bought the land from told us with such confidence and authority that we believed them," he replied.

"Okay, I hope it is all sorted out now," Mom asked.

"Oh yes. Please, just get your land papers – let us do one joint survey and check, just in case," Tony said.

"First, you break our wall. Now you want to check our papers. You have some nerve..." I was interrupted by mom: "When shall we do the survey?"

"Tomorrow...I will let you know when," he replied.

We went to the car. I asked mom why she had agreed instead of asking them to build our compound, or filing a police case. "Aryan, it's for a NGO...they must have been misled by the previous owners. Eswarappa Reddy was the previous owner; that family didn't get along with dad. So let's solve their doubt. You are almost a qualified civil engineer – I am sure you can handle this." As she was speaking, Dev collapsed near the car door.

"What happened to him?" I asked.

"He came home late last night – around 4a.m. I woke him up to bring him here. He must be tired."

I went to lift him up; he reeked of alcohol. Somehow, mom refused to believe he drank. She believed that her sons couldn't do anything wrong, and that everyone in the world was trying to corrupt us. We drove home and put Dev to sleep. Later that evening, Dev began to shiver violently. We drove him to the hospital. The doctor said he was sick due to excessive drinking. My mother told our nosy relatives and neighbours that it was food poisoning. I guess she was concerned about what others would think of our family. Husband in a vegetative state, sons are drunkards and rowdies...she was trying her best to keep up the family Image.

The next day, I called Tony. He told me that he was busy and had to re-schedule our survey. I began calling him daily, and this went on for more than 10 days. Finally, I asked my lawyer to intervene. Tony gave us a date. Dad was an IIT graduate in civil engineering – there was no way he would have made any mistake in the marking of the boundary. Anyway, I had to prepare for the survey, so I took out my surveying book and began to study with dedication. It was my family land, our last hope to leading a good life. I was not going to let this go by.

Sanjanna kept trying to meet me. I told her I was stuck in this deal and that it would get over soon. I continued to speak to her over the phone and in college during breaks. Soon, we fixed a day for the joint survey. The day before the survey, I went through all the documents that were stored in dad's steel cupboard. I came across a file with the label

'Police Cases' – they were police cases filed against my dad and legal documents of the proceedings. According to the case file, Eswarappa had sent his goons to push my dad out from the factory land. My dad, the decent IIT civil engineer, had whacked all of them single-handedly and chased them off the land. The so-called goons had asked the police for protection from my father and filed a case against him. He was soon arrested and released on bail.

Another case: At night, Eswarappa used to plant sandalwood trees in out compound to prove to the Collector that the factory working in that area would destroy those precious plants and destroy framing in the locality. Dad used to go for the late night show and, around 11p.m., go back to the factory and pull out those plants. *I wondered how dad managed to know when they were planning to plant the trees*. As I was thinking, dad came into the office; he saw the file I was reading.

"This file has nothing to do with your survey for tomorrow," he said.

I closed the file and gave it to him. "But how did you know when they were going to plant the trees?"

He closed the door and came and sat across me.

"Aryan, remember this – in any business, information is the most important resource you will have. He who gets the information first and puts it to the right use can reach the top." I saw a gleam in dad's eyes for the first time.

"So, how did you pull it off?" I asked him.

"After the first time he sent guys to chase me off the land, I placed one of our boys in his house as a labourer," he replied.

I was shocked – was my Dad as twisted as I was? Or was I twisted because this was genetics at work?

"Remember, Aryan, these guys are going to come at you from all different directions and they will use all means to threaten and entice you. Be smart and calm. I am behind you. When you need help to figure out things, speak to me. Don't bother your mother with details – she is little worried when it comes to these types of matters. Her family has never done business. They were rich landlords who kept eating into their inheritance till they all went broke."

He got up and left. This was the first time dad had given me advice. I felt a sense of pride. No wonder this man was dying; they had taken away his one favourite thing – business.

The next day, I was up early and ready for the survey. I reached the place at 9.30a.m. with a 50-metre tape and a book. They came only at 11a.m., with a group of 10 to 12 people. They had chai brought to them, and begun to have a little discussion. Then, they asked me, "Shall we start? Is your dad coming?"

"These are small things. Dad told me to take care of it," I replied.

They were offended by my comment, but didn't say anything. They introduced me to Robert, their surveyor. Everyone sat under a tree while Robert and I went around measuring the land. Eventually, he agreed that the area shown in our sale deed matched the on site measurements. All the NGO's members came up to me and apologised and said they would build back the compound – everyone except Tony.

I was happy. I went home and informed everyone. Dad called me to his room and asked me, "What exactly happened?" I told him everything, point by point. "So, they sat down while you were busy taking measurements?" He looked worried.

"Yes, Robert and I did the survey. The rest were sitting down and having chai."

"Aryan, this problem is not over. There is someone else playing. Be careful."

I wondered why the old man was so worried. I called up Sanjanna that night and went to the hostel to meet her. We went out for dinner.

"Why don't you ask Sahail to help you out?" she asked.

"No. He is still recovering from his drug abuse, and any tension could push him back."

"Why don't you ask your brother to help you out?"

"He is too young and I want him to keep out of trouble. What's wrong, honey? Why do you want someone to be with me?" I asked her.

'No, I am just worried about you, that's all. You helped these people. When you need help, they should help you, right?"

"I didn't help them looking at the fact that they would help back sometime," I said.

When I dropped her back and was about to leave, she held my hand and came close to me.

"When can we go to Sahail's place next?"

"Soon, very soon," I replied.

Next day, after college, I went to the factory and saw that they had begun to build their boundary but had not started building our compound wall. I called Tony; he told me they had started on one side to avoid unwanted entry into the property. After they finished that, they would begin on mine. Something was definitely fishy here. I waited for two more days, and then got our own labourers to build back our compound wall.

The moment we started work, all hell broke loose. Some guys came in a Sumo car and began to chase the labourers off the site. They did not speak to me. Soon, the site was empty except for me and the guys who came in the car. Then, they came up to me and said, "Boss wants to speak to you."

"Who? Tony?"

"No, Ramesh anna." Ramesh Reddy, son of Eswarappa Reddy.

I was taken aback. Dad had warned me that this had not ended and that someone was playing from behind the scene. They asked me to get into their vehicle. I refused and got into my own vehicle and followed them. I wanted to know what connection this person had with the NGO, other than selling the land to them.

After driving for a while through a narrow road we reached a small farmhouse. There were a few people standing outside and supervising the construction of a double-storied house beside the farm.

I got down from the car, and they led me to a short fellow with long hair. He introduced himself as Ramesh Reddy. He screamed at his men to get me a chair and some chai. We both sat down.

He began: "That land on which the NGO is building is my land."

"You sold it to them," I replied.

"No, my brother sold it to them. He has no right over the property as per our father's will."

"Okay, but I was building only my wall, which they had broken."

"By all means you can, but I need to verify first if that's my land or yours."

I gathered some courage and told him, "We have been on that land since the time your father was trying to grab the land."

He laughed. "So, Mr. Dutt has not yet retired. From what I heard, he was on his deathbed. So, he has already explained everything to his son. Listen carefully, boy – that land belonged to my family. Your father cheated us and took possession of that land."

"That land didn't belong to your family at all. I checked the family tree of that land – there is no mention of anyone from your family at all." The family tree depicts the ownership of the land before and how it came into being.

"My dad, the late Eswarappa, brought both the adjacent land parcels in hopes of buying that existing factory land from the previous owners. We almost had them giving up on the land, when your dad stepped in and registered the land at a very low cost from the previous owners."

"Still, how does that land become yours?"

"My grandfather wanted to build an engineering college in our locality. My dad invested and brought two acres on either side to the land in question, much before your dad came into the scene. As per government regulations, we needed a bigger land to start all branches, so we approached the previous owner for sale of their land – which they refused. We purchased the adjacent two acres in the hope that we would be able to get this land from her but that stubborn lady did not budge. We even burnt the crops she was growing there, but she did not budge. Finally, due to some financial crisis in her family, she was ready to sell. We offered an amount, but she didn't agree. We knew she would eventually agree as that was our area and no one would by the land we are interested in – except for your dad." He paused, took a sip of his chai, lit a smoke and continued.

"It was because of your dad that we had to put an end to our college dream, and that land was left empty. My father tried many times to get that land, but your father foiled his plans. Recently, we heard your land was up for sale. We sent our uncle to approach you for purchasing the land, but your mother was quoting too high a rate and she had a hundred terms and conditions. My dad told me to forget that land; he said it was never going to be ours. With that, he passed away without fulfilling his father's dream. But now, my friend, I have the upper hand. My brother is the ACP of police, and this locality comes under his jurisdiction. I have enough boys to break down your entire compound wall and claim that land as mine, but I want your dad to willingly part with that land..."

I began to laugh. "Why are you laughing?" he asked me, a little astonished.

"Just imagine – my dad thought of this as such a small problem that he sent me alone to solve it. He didn't even think it was worth his time," I told him.

"Laugh all you want, but that land belongs to me. Don't step on it – if not, my people will get physical with you."

"Physical? Why? Are they planning to rape me?" I asked with a smirk.

"Get out!" he yelled.

I went home and told dad, mom and Dev of everything that had happened. Mom began to panic – she told me to call the lawyer. I told her to calm down.

"How can I calm down? That is the last piece of land your father has. If that's gone, I don't know how we are going to afford anything anymore." She began to weep.

I told mom to stop crying. Later that night, while I was sitting in dad's old office room and contemplating on our next move, dad came into the room.

"Are you afraid?" he asked.

"A bit," I replied.

"Fear is good. It helps you think better," he said and left the room.

The next day, I took a foldable chair and went to the factory land. On my way there, I picked up a pack of cigarettes. Once I reached the site, I sat down on the chair. Soon, Ramesh's goons came and questioned me. I told them this was my land; if they laid a hand on me I would file a case of attempt to murder. They laughed and went away. Within five minutes, a police jeep came to the site, and a policeman arrested me for trespassing. I was taken to see the Sub Inspector, Mr. Harish. "Young man, why are you breaking the law and disturbing the peace?" he asked. He was definitely paid off by Ramesh. I thought of playing along.

"Sir, it is my father's land. What law did I break?"

"According to this family partition deed, that land belongs to Mr. Ramesh," he replied, waving Ramesh Reddy's partition deed.

"Sir, according to my family's partition deed, my grandfather wrote this police station in my name. Could you all please vacate the premises," I replied.

As soon as he heard my reply he began a verbal onslaught of abuses,just then a constable came into his room and asked me to follow him to the ACP's room. The Sub Inspector shouted, "Can't you see I am questioning him? How dare you come into my room without permission and take this fellow away without even asking for my permission?"

"Sorry sir, ACP sir told me to get him to his cabin immediately," the constable replied.

"That fellow has just taken charge and is already trying to show his power with me. Wait, I will teach him a lesson. Take him and go!" Harish shouted.

I walked into the ACP cabin. "What's your name, son?" he asked.

"Aryan."

"I overheard your story," he said and laughed.

He was a newly appointed ACP, and his name was Mr. Gupta. He asked me to sit and explain the problem. I did. Finally, he told me to file a case against Ramesh as this was a civil matter; it would be taken up in court. I told him that we would file a case directly in the court. He agreed and let me leave. Why I did not file a police case against Ramesh, I did not know, but I guess I didn't trust the police after the incident with Chottu.

A couple of days after the police station incident, we got a court notice. Mr. Ramesh had filed a caveat that, in other terms, meant the court could not pass any order without informing him. Dev took off from college; mom called the lawyer and friends who had dealt with such cases before. I began checking the Net on the effects of this notice. The only person who calmly went about his daily routine was dad. After getting ready, he sat in the living room and gazed out of the window. I went up to him and said, "He has sent us a notice."

"Good. It has begun," he replied.

"Aren't you worried?"

"Aryan, that's my land and will be my land, no matter what notice he sends. They cannot fold up the land and put it into their pocket. And tell your mother to stop panicking. It is 8 in the morning – no lawyer is going to take your call. Those fellows wake up at 10 in the morning and go to sleep by 5 in the evening. Ask her to get breakfast ready."

I was flummoxed; later, I understood that 10a.m. to 5p.m. were the court timings.

"Ma, dad asked you to prepare breakfast." Her eyes flared as she banged the phone down and went to have a word with Dad.

Dad sat there calmly. After mom finished shouting, he asked her, "Do you want me to buy breakfast and come?"

Mom walked out of the room, mumbling, "This man and his food! People are on fire here and he sits calmly and looks out of the window."

We went up to Dad. "Dad, I don't think you understand the situation here."

"Boys, grow up. No point in getting worried when you need to be calm. For the past half-an-hour, I am seeing all of you running around, calling this person and that person. What did you achieve, other than telling the whole word you are having a problem? Relax, eat a good breakfast, take the notice and go the lawyer's office. He will explain what needs to be done. These things don't get done or undone at the snap of a finger. You will understand patience once you fellows start going to the court. Now, shut up and relax till breakfast is ready."

The lawyer office reminded me of a 1950s movie set. Everything looked black and white, and his table was filled with many files. People in his office moved at their own pace. We ran into his room with the notice. He asked us to sit down; "Let me finish my breakfast. I come and meet you." It was 9.30a.m. At 9.45, he came out and asked, "Mr. Dutt's sons, right?"

"Yes," Dev replied.

"Okay. What happened?"

We explained to him about the notice.

"Oh, this is nothing. He knows that we are going to file a case against him, so the court will have to inform him before passing any order. Don't worry."

"So, when are we filing the case?" I asked.

"Hopefully today...I am waiting for my junior to come. He will file the case for you."

"Junior? Aren't you our lawyer?" I asked him.

"Aryan, I don't enter the court. Your father knows that. I had an argument with a judge over a wrong verdict he had delivered many years back, after which I have never entered the court or worn my robe."

Dev and I looked at each other. We went home.

"Are you aware that Mr. Francis, your lawyer, does not go to court?" I asked Dad.

"Yes, I am aware. Why?" he asked me.

"You want to hire a guy who does not enter the court, but send some juniors for a serious case like this?" I argued.

"He has more knowledge than many other people I know regarding civil disputes. That hair didn't become grey just like that," dad said and laughed. "Boys, everyone knows what the law is, and we are on the right. For a case like this, you need someone who is honest, not over-smart."

Old people and their loyalties. I really did not understand why we could not hire one of those dashing lawyers.

Finally, all the documentation was done. When we went to file the case, his junior, Mr. Thomas, asked me to pay some money to the guy who was taking the case papers. I quietly paid him. Later, I asked Thomas, "Why did we need to pay him?"

"Because I have asked for the case papers to be submitted in court No. 10 only," he replied.

"Why?"

"My boss asked me to do that."

Back at Francis's office, I asked our lawyer, "Why did we need the case to be filed in court No. 10 only?"

"Aryan, for a case like this, it helps to find a tough, no nonsense and honest judge."

"Is it not their duty to be fair and honest?"

"My boy, the law is such that it depends on what is told and how the judge reads into it, or whether he wants to read in to it at all. Let me give you an example. In one of the cities in the USA, a fire broke out in an apartment building and all the residents were evacuated. Suddenly, they heard a scream of a little Kid. Out of nowhere, a person ran into the apartment building and, five minutes later, came out with a something wrapped in a quilt. All of them were happy and began to clap, thinking that he had rescued the baby. When he unwrapped the quilt, it was a locker box. When they questioned him on why did he not save the baby, he replied that this was his life savings for which he ran into the fire to retrive.

"Now, Aryan, imagine that the man had died when he ran inside. The whole country would have awarded him for bravery, as they would have thought he had gone to save the little baby. The truth was revealed only when he came back out. Does it make him guilty? No – he was just protecting his interest. Is he a bad person? Yes, in my opinion, but not in the eyes of the law. So, it depends on who hears your plea and how he wants to interpret what you say." I merely nodded.

In court, the first process is to prove that you are who you say you are. You have to make an affidavit stating that you are who you say you are, and some guy who has never seen you before will gaze at you from top to bottom and then decided how much to charge you to prove you are you! I apparently cost Rs. 50. Along with this, you submit the land documents and other legal papers. The first date was set on 14 April, 2002.

Sanjanna and I had not met since this case started. Ghoush called me often, but I did not confide in him or anyone else. I didn't trust anyone at this point. I doubted whether I was devoting myself a hundred percent to protect my family land. Sanjanna and I talked on the phone. I told her to give me some time until the case got over – then, I would be all hers.

On 14 April, I reached the lawyers office by 9.30a.m. It was closed. Soon, Thomas called me and told me to come to court. He had another court case; I asked him about mine.

"You wait in the court. If they call your case, say you are present. That's all."

"What?"

"Don't worry. If they ask for your lawyer, tell I have another hearing at Court 5 and will come soon."

Before I could say anything, he ended the call. I reached the court and saw a chart stuck outside. It was like an examination results list. I saw our case close to the top position and felt happy thinking that we were successful. I realised this was a court order list, not a results list. As the case drew closer, I called the lawyer. As I was listening to the record note of his voice mail, someone grabbed my phone – it was a cop. He told me I was not allowed to use a phone in the court premises. He switched it off and returned it to me.

Soon, my case was called: "O.S No 124534/2002 Mr. Dutt Vs Mr. Ramesh Reddy." I stood up and went to the front; along with me, the other party's lawyer stood up. We walked up to the judge.

"Where is your lawyer?"

"He is in Court 5 and will come soon."

"What about you? Where is your client?" He asked the defense lawyer.

"Sir, he has not come. I am representing him." he replied.

"What do you have to say?" he asked the lawyer.

"Sir, that land belongs to my client and we need a few days to reply to the case filled By Mr. Dutt."

"Okay, I will move the case to 21 April, 2002."

I nodded. Ramesh's lawyer objected: "Sir, we require more time than that."

"Why? Are you manufacturing those documents?" the judge asked sarcastically.

That statement put a smile on my face, which was wiped out with his next statement: "And you – next time, see that your lawyer is present here."

"Yes, your honour."

Soon, Thomas came over and asked, "What happened?"

"We won the case," I replied angrily.

"Aryan, sorry for being late. Tell me what happened."

"It is pushed to 21 April."

He jotted down the date and went to speak to the attender who was dealing with the files. He came up to me and said, "The opposition lawyer is Mr. Radhakrishna. He is known for his crooked ways. We must watch out."

I went back home. As soon as I entered, mom asked me, "What happened? Is everything alright?"

"Yes. They asked for more time, so the next hearing is on 21 April," I replied

My dad, who was sitting in a corner, said, "The next hearing is quite fast. Lucky fellow."

I was pleased with myself.

In the days between the court cases, I would go and sit alone on the factory land after college. Ramesh's goons also sat on the land. I had no interaction with my friends; I did not want to talk to my girlfriend. The case and its outcome became an obsession for me. This was my family's last chance to become rich again.

One day, Sanjanna called me. "Can we meet for lunch tomorrow? My dad wants to meet you."

"What? You told your dad about us?" This was the worst timing possible.

"Yes...sort of...please come."

The next day, I shaved, dressed and went to college. During the lunch break, I went to a restaurant called Hopes to meet her father, the famous Dr. Rao. They were already there, waiting for me.

"Hi!" I waved to Sanjanna. She waved back and gestured towards their table. She introduced me to her father; I greeted him and sat down. He did not look happy. As the lunch progressed, he ignored me. Soon, it was time to go back to college. He paid the bill and we walked out. When I turned to leave, he said, "Aryan, stay for some time. I need to talk to you. Sanjanna, you carry on. I will meet you after your college." Sanjanna seemed doubtful but she left.

Her father turned toward me and asked, "What do you think you doing?"

"What?"

"Why you playing the fool with my daughter?"

"Sir, I am not playing the fool. I am in love with her and she is with me."

"What does your father do?"

"He is retired, sir."

"I inquired about your family; you are barely making ends meet."

" I don't understand how that affects the relationship between me and your daughter."

"How are you planning to take care of my daughter?"

"I will earn like the rest and make ends meet."

"Yes Aryan, all you can do is to make ends meet."

"Sir, what is the real problem here?"

"Aryan, just leave her. She is not meant for you."

"Sir, I have to go. And I am not going to leave her...I love her..."

That evening, I told Sanjanna about what had happened; I wanted her to know how her family felt about me.

She said, "He is just protective, that's all. Don't worry; he will soon get to know you like I have."

9. Case in Progress

Soon, the case began to pick up pace and the judge was shooting down their requests for more time. I began to wonder if they knew that we had signed an agreement with Mr. Chetty for sale. I spoke to the builder and he assured me there was no hurry. Meanwhile, Ramesh began to use force against us. His goons once pulled me by the collar and asked me not to enter the land any more. I did not respond, even though I wanted to punch the guy. I understood that these people were trying to delay or stall the case, and since that was not working, they were trying to make it a criminal case so as to complicate it and blackmail my family into releasing the land. I swallowed my pride and stood there without retaliating. The next time I went to the factory, they began to urinate on the spot I sat. I controlled my temper. The land belonged to my father and I was not going to let them take it away.

Exams were upon me. I was juggling a lot. I had not met any of my friends or Sanjanna for days. Just before the exams began, Sanjanna called me. "Aryan, we need to talk."

"Now what happened?"

"I don't think this relationship is working out."

"Sanjanna, hold on for some more time. I just need to finish this for the family. After that, I will be free."

"It's always family or friends. You never have time for me."

"I love you, Sanjanna. Don't say that."

"No! Aryan, it's over."

"Sanjanna, hold on. Let me come over and talk to you."

"No need, Aryan; my father was right about you."

"Your father was right? Didn't you say he would soon know me the way you know me?" I lost my cool and shouted at her.

"The way you shouting at me – that is your true nature. You are a goonda and it was bound to show up sooner or later!"

"What bullshit! You were with this goonda for two years, and now you feel there is a problem. I am coming there to talk to you."

"I am not at the hostel. I am at Nikhil's house with my friends to study."

I slammed the phone down. I was in a rage. I could not believe that she broke up with me –over the phone, in front of her friends.

I wanted to scream, but I could not. I did not want my family to know what was happening in my life. There was already too much tension in the house. Suddenly, I saw my books. A thought ran through my head – that girl thought she was better than me in studies; if I scored better marks than her, she would come back. I began to study like I had never studied before. When I needed a break, I went to see the lawyer to see the progress of the case. I did not shave or cut my nails. I looked like a beast. I did not care. She did not call. The exams got over and I continued to follow up on the case. The judge began to tighten the noose around the defendant.

Soon, we started to get threatening calls on the landline. I stopped going out totally. I stayed at home as I was afraid they would harm my family. One day, Pawan, my friend from school came to my house and asked me to join him for a smoke. As I was leaving my house, I saw the group of goons that used to sit on the land coming towards my house. I closed the gate and went up to them. "What do you want, benchod?" I asked them. They were shocked by my question, and the way I looked.

"We want to discuss with your father and resolve the issue."

"You little fucks think I will let you talk to my father? After this case is over, I will come after each one of you."

Pawan came in at that time. "What's happening here?" he asked.

"Who are you?" they asked him

"I am ex-Chief Justice Govindraju's grandson."

They mellowed down. They told him about the case and how they wanted to settle the matter. Pawan said, "You want to fight against this fellow? Be careful – he will not forget this even after the case gets over. He will come after each and every one of you guys. I speak from experience." Slowly, the group broke up and they left.

"Aryan, what's happening? Why didn't you tell me?" Pawan asked me.

"I didn't know who to tell what. Anyways, it is soon coming to an end. The final hearing is on 15th June."

"Let me know about the court verdict; I can speak to my dad and help you guys out."

We had a smoke together and then parted ways.

On 15th June, the verdict was read out. I did not understand a word. I asked my lawyer what had happened. He told we had won the case – the other party had to rebuild the compound and police was directed to enforce the order. I was ecstatic! I called my family and informed them. They were very happy. I felt like I had achieved my goal, but now what?

10. Trouble In The Family

Soon, the land was sold and we received the money. We did not know what to do with that much money. Mom suggested that we put it in a fixed account and collect interest; I suggested buying some land as it had the best appreciation value. Mom was against any land dealings, so I suggested buying an apartment. She was still very doubtful. After some research, I narrowed down on one apartment. Dad and I finished the formalities. When I came back, mom asked my how much did it had come up to including registration, lawyer fees and other formalities.

"88 lakhs," I replied.

"That's a lot! I don't think that apartment is worth so much money."

"Don't worry mom. It's an investment that will grow."

"No Aryan, I think you were hasty in this purchase. I think you should step aside. You can't go on spending the family's money like this."

"I didn't buy anything for myself, mom. I brought an apartment in dad's name, not mine," I retorted.

"Still, you should leave all decisions from now on to your dad and me."

I walked out of the room. Was she kidding me? I fought for this family. I gave up my social life, friends, everything.

I ran around for the entire case – now, she was telling me to back off.

After a few days, I asked mom for two lakhs. I had promised to donate that amount to the temple once the case was settled.

"No, Aryan. That's not your money to promise anything."

"What?" I asked.

"Yes. It belongs to the family."

"Where was Dev when all of this was going on? He was busy getting drunk and you were busy worrying. I fought this case and won. I stood up to those fellows and won. I stood tall for this very same family!"

"No more arguments. You're just a kid," she said.

Dev butted in: "Why do you get to do what you want with the money and decide what we should buy? Who made you the boss?"

I turned to my father for support, but he had his face turned towards his favourite window.

I walked away. I was heartbroken. I needed to talk to someone. I called Sanjanna.

"Sanjanna, we won the case."

"Oh, I am happy for you. Good you called – I wanted to tell you something."

"What?"

"Don't lose your cool, okay. I am dating Nikhil…I think I love him."

My heart sank. This was turning out to be the worst day of my life. I drove around the city aimlessly. I decided to go towards the factory. I sat in front of the factory, lit up a cigarette and puffed away. I decided to get drunk to calm the storm brewing inside of me. There was an old abandoned quarry close by to the factory; on the way there, I stopped at a wine store and picked up some drinks. When I came out, I saw Ghoush Khan. He walked up to me. "What happened, bhai?"

"Nothing. Just going for a drink at the quarry."

"I will come with you."

We rode out there. I sat down and began to drink. I was completely broken. What was my purpose in life? I stood by my family all these days. The girl whom I had loved left me because I favoured my family more than her. I had avoided my friends so that I could concentrate on wining the case, so that land could be sold and Dev could be educated aboard. That very same brother had backstabbed me today and Sanjanna has fallen in love with her friend.

Khan sat quietly for a long time. Then, he said, "Bhai, we have seen your girlfriend getting close to that Nikhil fellow."

"Yes! She is now in love with him." I laughed bitterly.

"Shall we do something?"

"Do something? What can we do other than sit and clap our hands, like my father? He saw everything but just sat there clapping his hands."

"Bhai, you are drunk. Let me drop you home."

"Home! What fucking home? Nobody wants me! You know why I wanted to come here today, Khan?"

I paused and stared at the deep gorge below us. "That is where I should be, at the bottom, if you had not tagged along."

"Don't worry, we can send you there," somebody said.

I quickly turned around to find Ramesh's boys walking towards me.

Soon, one of them, Babu, came in front of me and yelled, "You thought we would let you and your family enjoy your new earned money?" He slapped me hard on my face. I could not lift my hand. There was something inside me that wanted to get beaten up. I wanted the physical pain to numb the pain that was within me. Ghoush rushed at them. They caught him by his hands and pinned him to the ground. Soon, all of them began to beat me. I was bleeding, cut and broken both emotionally and physically. I lost the will to react. *Let these fellows kill me. I think I lost the real me. Compromising at every step for family and love, I lost the real me.* Soon everything began to fade away. When I eventually woke up, I was at the hospital. Ghoush was in the bed next to mine.

"Bhai, who where those people?"

"Don't call me bhai anymore."

Soon, dad and mom came. "Now you started to get into fights?" mom asked me.

"I did not get into any fight; Ramesh's people did this to me."

"You smell of liquor. You must have instigated the fight."All of a sudden her sense of smell was back on track.

I looked at my dad, but he was silent. The cops came to take my report. Sub Inspector Harish came. With a grin on his face, he asked me, "How did you fall down?"

"I did not fall down. I was beaten up," I replied.

"No officer, he fell down," mom insisted.

I looked at her with disgust. I knew she did not want another case. I was the scapegoat that was scarified to maintain peace. She spoke to the officer and sent him away. While he was leaving, he looked at me and smiled.

"We don't need that kind of trouble. It's over; let's close the matter," mom argued.

"Close the matter? Look at me! They left me for dead and you want them to get away?" I shouted.

"You have a younger brother. If you file a case today, they will attack him tomorrow!"

"Talking of my younger brother, where is he?" I asked sarcastically.

"He is in college. He will come later," mom replied.

During my time in hospital, I got close to Khan.

"Don't you feel lonely, Khan?" I asked him.

"I have been alone from birth. My parents died when I was born. I live with my father's brother. He takes care of me but when it comes to his own family's welfare, I am set aside," he replied.

"How come he put you in engineering? It must be expensive."

"I am an investment for them. They want me to get into the Public Works department so I can take money under the table and make them rich. My uncle's son is in London, studying management. They want him to get a white collar job."

I laughed at the miseries of life. Ten days, two fractures and seventeen stitches later, I was discharged. Khan left earlier. No one from college or school, not even Sahail, came to see me in hospital. Dev came to pick me up. I didn't speak a word to him. After a few days, Ghoush Khan came home and met me.

"Bhai, that fellow is openly walking around college with your girlfriend. It's time to do something."

"No Khan." I replied.

"Why? And what about the people who attacked us in the quarry?"

"No...Nobody...While I lay in the hospital, not a single person came to meet me or enquire about me. Do you know why?"

"No."

"Nobody gives a damn about me. Nobody respects me."

"Respect?"

"Yes. I have to earn that respect."

"But how?"

"Money, Khan, money! The one and only thing that commands respect. We need to make lots and lots of money – quickly. After that, one by one, I will settle all scores."

"How do we make money?"

"Khan, all we need is a stubborn heart...money will quietly follow us. We have to wait for the right opportunity." I took a sip of water. "First, I need to finish my engineering course with flying colours."

"Why do you need to do that?" asked a confused Ghoush Khan.

"You will understand soon," I replied.

Soon, I was able to walk. I distanced myself from everybody in college and at home. I began to attend classes regularly. During breaks, I stayed in class. Khan gave me company. We went out for a smoke once in a while. One such day, I saw Sanjanna leaving with Nikhil in his car. My anger rose and my eyes became red, but I could not move. Khan saw me and understood what I was feeling. He hopped onto his bike and chased after Nikhil's car. I chased after him to prevent him from doing anything crazy. Khan had cornered Nikhil's car with his bike. He got down from the bike and walked towards the car; Nikhil rolled down his window to shout at Khan. Khan pulled Nikhil out through the window and threw him to the ground. I ran over, and pushed Khan off Nikhil. Sanjanna stepped out of the car.

"Aryan! What's going on here? Who is this guy? What do you think you're doing?"

"Shut up and get back in the car. And take this pussy with you," I snapped at her.

She was shocked, but she got into the car with Nikhil and left.

"Why did you let them go, bhai?"

"I am not letting anyone go. It is not yet time."

I walked away and a disgruntled Ghoush followed me. I avoided Sanjanna for the remainder of my college days. I finished college with an aggregate of 76 percent. She finished with 64 percent. I called her.

"What is your aggregate?" I asked.

"What? You called to ask me that?"

"Yes."

"64 percent."

"I got 76 percent. I am not some goonda. I am much smarter and can achieve more in life than you ever will. Remember what you told me – that my mother expects too much? She knows her son's capability."

"Aryan, I didn't mean to..."

"Too late...bye." I hung up the phone.

She called me many times, but I did not answer. Khan managed to scrape through the examinations. He came home that evening. I sat on his bike.

"Where to, bhai?"

"Quarry."

He looked at me disbelievingly. "Start the bike and move."

On the way, I picked up some liquor. I began to drink in the very same place I had received a sound thrashing for protecting my family. The same family that did not do anything to protect or avenge me.

"Now what, bhai?"

"We need to amass money and power."

"How?"

"Illegally."

We were graduates waiting for a right opportunity. "Have you applied for any job?" I asked Khan.

"No bhai. What is the use? Our seniors have been sitting idle for the past two years without a job...markets were dull. Now, the markets have picked up and companies have begun recruiting, but they are rejecting people without experience."

"So, if they don't have any past experience, they don't get a job?"

"Bhai, now the job market has picked up, but previously it was really bad for all fields. So, guys like me, who did not pass in first class, could not get a decent job. Now, they still cannot get a job because the company needs previous work history."

"Print something and give it to them."

"No. The company HR checks on the credentials submitted and the credibility of all your certificates. If you are found cheating, they can have you arrested and then inform all the other companies to stay away from you."

"Poor guys. They are stuck, I suppose."

"They are ready to pay any amount to get a decent job, but I guess its fate..."

Suddenly, an idea hit me. I asked Ghoush to take me home. I went straight into my room and was busy browsing the Internet. I printed out a few sheets and jotted down notes on blank sheets of paper. I fell asleep at the table, after working late into the night.

The next day Ghoush and I went to a park. I took out the printed notes and writings.

"What is this, bhai?"

"Path to success," I replied.

"What?"

"Remember, you told me that guys without jobs are willing to pay for good character certificate and previous employer's letter of recommendation?"

"Yes, but they will also do a background check."

"Let them. What if we are a registered company that is open for only issuing documents required for people to get new jobs."

"It's risky, bhai, but I think this might work."

11. Risky Business

We began to work towards our goal. First, we had to collect all the information that a human resource teams collects. For a trial run, we fixed up Ghoush Khan's cousin Arif, who already had a job, for an interview with another company. As expected, within a few days, we received a call regarding Arif. It worked! Soon, we collected money for providing fake certificates and number.

We took the money and opened a registered company called Creative Solutions in Hennur town. We registered it under civil and IT. This became our front for fake experience certificates. We had six landline numbers and 10 mobile numbers. We divided them according to civil and IT. The candidates' files and documents were properly arranged. We even arranged for ID badges for candidates to impress their interviewer.

Business began to grow. I hired a receptionist named Divya. She was aware of what was going on, and was willing to take the risk for extra money. Money began to pour in. We charged between Rs. 8,000 and Rs. 25,000, depending on the person's requirements. We began to make lakhs within a month.

Ghoush was in charge of daily operations. I began to set up shops in Hyderabad, Chennai and Kerala. Before I did this, I went to meet ACP Gupta of Hennur station – the same person who had advised me about Ramesh. I told him everything.

"Aryan, you know what you are doing is illegal and risky?"

"Sir, that's why we need you, we will see that your share reaches your home every month. Our only condition is that if our boys ever get caught, they should get back to their families the very same day. I have kept one suitcase in your car outside as a token from our side."

He smiled. Later, Ghoush asked me how much I had given him.

"Five lakhs."

"Why did you pay him so much?"

"I may have other needs for him soon. Now, I am out of operations and you are in charge – all legal hassles end with you. I have passed on all ownership to you. Come home every week and give me the accounts personally – never on the phone."

My parents were aware that I had opened an office, but did not know the full details. I had shifted out of my parent's home to a double-bedroom flat that I had brought with our profits. One year later, we had a profit of 60 lakhs. Profits were mostly in black. I spoke to Ghoush and told him to started lending the money on interest. We also recruited more boys to handle collections. No one knew I was involved fully with the company; they were always made to believe that I was more of an investor. The money lending business did have some problems, but I got ACP Gupta to partner with us on that too. Soon, payments began to flow in. I needed to become rich soon, and I was ready to do anything to make that happen. One day, Khan and I were sitting in my apartment and drinking when ACP Gupta called.

"Where are you, Aryan?"

"At home. Why?"

"Wait there. I am coming to meet you."

I told Khan to clean up the living room and open up the windows. ACP Gupta was accompanied by a gentleman named Gomes. He was into import and export.

"Tell me, sir, what bring you to my humble apartment?" I asked as I poured them both a drink.

"Aryan, one of his packages is stuck in the customs godown in Cochin. We need you to get it out of there for him."

I looked at Ghoush; he shut the windows.

"What's in it?"

"That is confidential," Gomes replied.

"Mr. Gomes, trust is all we have. I need to know what I have to get out for you before I decide to do it."

He was hesitant when he spoke: "It's a large box with black paper."

"Black paper?"

"They are American dollars that have been smuggled into India. We have coated it with a chemical that keeps the officers from identifying the currency and the country it is from. Only we have the reversal process."

"What is the value?"

"10 million dollars," said Gomes.

"That's 50 crore rupees," said Gupta.

"What's our commission?" I asked.

"2 percent."

"Okay," I replied.

Gomes was taken aback. "You are not going to haggle with me?" he asked.

"Sir, this is just the start of our relationship. Today, I help you; tomorrow, you help me. Money goes around, that's all."

"You are young, but you really know how to win a friend," Gomes said.

"Please give us all the details so we can make our preparations."

Gomes told us it was a large black box with an eagle seal on the outside of the box. I told him to leave his number and to give us a few days. They finished their drinks and left.

"Khan, pour me a drink, yaar." I walked out to the balcony.

"Bhai, this is risky work. Why did you agree to take this?"

"Khan, we need to grow fast. This is a perfect job to mark our entry into the big league."

"How are we going to do this?"

"Get me a fake driver's license, and book my ticket to Cochin by train through a travel agency under that false driver's name."

"I am coming with you."

"Khan, I need someone outside. If things go wrong, who will handle the company?"

Khan was disappointed, but he knew my answer was final. I began to think about how I was going to break in and get that box. I left for Cochin. I checked into a cheap hotel – one that did not have camera. The next day I went to the customs godown, and scouted the place. When I was questioned, I informed them I had come to fill the tender forms. While waiting in the hall, I saw an article on the notice board – it was about a customs officer in Mumbai who had risked his life and captured a smuggler.

I called Ghoush. "I need you to make a customs ID badge with my photo. Name will be Ajay Sharma and designation will be senior officer." He had it couriered to me within a few days.

The next day after I received the courier from Khan, I went to the customs house in Cochin.

"I am Ajay Sharma from Mumbai branch. I have come to meet Mr. Garg," I told the security guards as I flashed my badge. They stood up and saluted me. I went to Mr. Garg's room and informed his PA to tell him that I have come from Mumbai on a confidential matter.

I was called in. I entered and saluted him. Behind the old desk sat a pot-bellied man who looked like he had never lifted his finger – not even to make a call.

"Yes?"

"Sir, I have come to inspect the box your team recovered from the smugglers last week."

"What box?" he asked quizzingly

"The box you are holding is actually a part of a large hawala scam we busted in Mumbai last month."

"Yes, yes, I remember. What's your name again?"He looked suprised

"Co. Ajay Sharma, sir."

"Yes, I remember. Your article was in the newspaper. Please sit down."

He asked his PA to bring some coffee and snacks.

"Yes, Ajay. How can we help?"

"Sir, I need to inspect that box and its contents."

"You know the rules. Get the required permission and come."

"Sir, we don't have time. I have already informed my seniors, but you know how our system works. It takes time. In fact, I have asked for this box to be transferred to the Mumbai godown so that all evidence is in one place. The order will be here soon."

"But, without orders, I can't help you, son."

"Sir, don't you want to share the credit for busting the biggest hawala racket in India?"

I had his attention. He agreed to let me inspect the box's contents.

"All have been blackened, so we don't know how much there is. My rough calculation is that it should be 10 million, if they are 100 dollars," he said, lifting up the notes.

"Wow! You have caught the mother load!" I exclaimed.

He was happy to hear that. We went back to his office. The tea had come by then. I went to wash my hands. When I came back, I told him to do the same, as the black chemical coating could be poisonous. When he went in to wash his hands, I added a chemical to his tea. Five minutes after drinking the tea, his stomach was upset. He excused himself and went to the bathroom. This time, I took out a few copies of his letter pad and took photos of his seal. I cut the telephone line and sat back in my chair. He came out.

"I think my stomach is upset."

"Sir, it might be that black coating. I know the remedy as I have had this problem before."

"What is it?"

"Please get some soda water, salt and lime I will make the concoction for you."

He picked up the receiver to call his PA, but the phone was dead.

He slammed the phone down.

"Sir, you relax. I will arrange for everything."

I went out and told his PA to get the file for goods transfer, and some soda, lime and salt. She gave me a quizzical look.

"Your boss wants them. And his telephone is not working. Check it."

She tried his extension; it was engaged. She came back into the room with me and asked, "Sir, do you need..." Before she could finish, he screamed, "Yes, yes! Get it fast!"

She ran out and he ran back into the toilet. I went to the toilet door and spoke to him: "Sir, you stay there. Once the items come, I will call you."

She came back with the file and went to get the other items. I opened his computer, typed the letter after looking at his previous goods transfer orders, and took a printout on his own letterhead. I sealed it. Now, I only needed his signature. I went back to my seat.

Soon, the lady came back with the other items. I mixed lots of salt in the soda, squeezed in a little lime, and called him back to the room. I made him drink it all in one gulp. He felt like vomiting and ran back to the bathroom. When he came out, he was feeling much better; his stomach was cleaned out.

"Ajay, I am leaving for the day. When you get the order, come and meet me," he said.

"Sure, sir. Take care." We walked out together.

I began to snoop around Cochin for someone who could fake signatures. One day, the bellboy of the hotel, who brought me my drinks, saw the blank sheet of paper on which I was trying to forge the signature. He picked up the paper and told me, "Sir, I know ...man...who...to do sign." He made a gesture with his hand .He took me to a village close to Cochin. We went to a shop that had wooden foldable shutters. It was closed from the outside. He knocked and spoke something in the local language. Somebody opened the door from the inside. We went through a passage and reached a dark, dingy room that was lit by an old oil candle. There were many documents in one shelf; on the other end was a lab. Amidst this sat an old man, who was reading a document with a magnifying glass. On his table where numerous pens and ink bottles of various brands. I knew I was in the right place.

"What can I do for you?"

I took out the letter of the customs officer and the photo of his signature on a previous order and placed it on his table. He looked through the document and saw the signature.

"You think with this letter they will let you take the goods out?"

"Yes," I replied.

"You will straight land in jail. There is a process in shifting out the items. Can't be done with this single paper," he said.

What did this old man know about these kinds of jobs?

"Sit down. We will get your items out." While speaking to me, he tore the papers. I lost my cool. "What are you doing?" I shouted.

"This is evidence that you were up to mischief, so I am destroying it." He turned to his aide and told him to call Roy. An hour later, a customs officer came into his den. They spoke for a while with the old man pointing to me. Then, they went into another chamber. Soon, Roy emerged from the room, stared at me and walked away. The old man called me into his chambers.

"So, you were planning to whisk away 50 crores with one letter?" He began to laugh. "Do you know that they have found you out, and are actually trying to nab you?"

"How?"

"Did you think that the PA appointed by the senior officer is dumb? She informed her boss about the file you asked for. Out of suspicion, Mr. Garg called Mumbai and found out about the real Ajay Sharma. This drama of yours has caused a stir in their office. They have decided to shift the box to Mumbai tomorrow by flight."

I was shocked and worried. *What about my word to Gomes?*

"Don't worry. Before it reaches the flight, the box will be with you. Question is, how much are you willing to pay?"

"You tell me?"

"One crore. In cash."

That was about how much I would get for completing the deal. I agreed on one condition –delivery was to be done in Bangalore, and payment would be done there. The next day, by noon, I took a flight back to Bangalore. The following day, the old man called me and gave me an address. I called Gomes and we went to Hotel Lake Plaza, room 303. The old man's aide opened the door. The old man was sitting there; the box was on the table. We opened the box, and took out a note. Gomes squeezed some chemical on the note and rubbed it in; the black vanished and it became a 100-dollar bill. He took out some random notes and did the same. He was very happy.

"Aryan, here, as promised," He handed over a bag to me. I passed it on to Ghoush Khan, who opened and verified the contents.

"Aryan, if you need any favour, please don't hesitate to call me." He closed the box and his people carried it away. He shook hands with me and left the room. I took the bag and handed it over to the old man.

"You charged that fellow only one crore?"

"Yes," I replied as I lit a cigarette.

"How come you agreed to pay me one crore? Didn't you think of yourself?"

"Sir, this business runs on name and word. I gave my word, so I would keep it even if I had to lose money. That's how your earn respect in this business."

"I like the way you think, son," he replied.

We exchanged a hug, and then Khan and I left the place. The entire trip was a waste according to my calculation – but little did I know that this particular dealing had made me so famous in Kerala and Karnataka that people with various problems began to approach me. I became a mediator between the government and people who had issues with the government. Money and power began to grow. I brought a palatial house in Hennur; I had a band of bodyguards and a line of super-luxury cars.

One day, while sitting in the balcony, Khan said, "Bhai, now you have money. You can buy anything you want."

"I think its time to buy some 'revenge'," I replied. "I think it's time to find out what our friend Ramesh has been up to. I want all details of every guy who raised his hand on us that day."

"Bhai, I have been keeping track of all those fellows. Ramesh has finally started his engineering college. He is still involved in land grabbing, but further up in Kothunur where his friend the Sub Inspector, now Inspector, Harish is in charge. He has two sons. But Ramesh was recently admitted to hospital for paralysis. He can hear and understand but can't move or talk. Babu, his right hand man, has moved out on his own. He identifies weak and problematic lands and strikes a deal to create problems later. The other three fellows work for Babu as his aides – even Robert, who did the survey on your factory land, is a part of Babu's team."

"Khan, it's time."

"What have you planned?"

"We start from the bottom and work our way to the top. Let's start with Babu and his aides."

Babu's aides brought him information about lands that were bound up in litigation or bought from a family in despair. To catch these animals, I had to lay a trap. I brought three acres of land for three cores in Divya's name. She was more than willing to help. Soon after the deal was done, we began to spread the message of how the person who had bought the land had died and his wife was now trying to sell it. This message was picked up by Babu's aides. He went to Divya's house to finalise the deal. They planned to give her a token advance and get her signature on the agreement. Once that was done, they would drag the payments till she went to court, and then harass her till she agreed for peanuts in settlement. Babu was well trained by his boss.

"Madam, what amount are you are looking for?" Babu asked.

"I don't have anything anymore. I want to sell the land and wind up all dealing here and go to America to settle with my brother." Divya replied.

"Very good, madam. What is your asking price?" He knew she did not have time.

"One crore and twenty lakhs per acre."

"Madam, that's very high! Market rate is 80 lakhs for one acre."

"Mr. Babu, this is my rate. Whoever matches this offer can buy the land from me."

"What is the advance amount?"

"Fifty percent at time of agreement."

That would be 60 lakhs for each acre. Total cost was one crore and eighty lakhs. He would lay down all his money on this deal. If he managed to chase this lady off the land and close it with another fifty lakhs, he stood to gain 70 lakhs, not considering the appreciation value that comes with time.

"Madam, please reconsider. I am ready to purchase, but reduce it a bit."

"One crore and fifteen lakhs is what I can reduce to for an acre. Total is three crores and forty-five lakhs. Advance is one core and seventy lakhs. Do you agree?"

"Madam, please make the advance one core."

"No, that will be difficult."

"Madam, anyway I will purchase the land from you within a month, so please bring down the advance."

"Okay."

"Madam, how much in black (cash) and white (DD)?"

"Fifty-fifty. Is it okay?"

"Yes. I will set up a date for signing the agreement and prepare the papers."

"Thank you." She shook hands and sent him away.

A few days later, she was asked for the date. She called me. "Sir, Babu called to fix a date. What date should I give?"

"Just hold on...Khan, when did we plan the other thing for?"

"26th of this month."

"Tell him 26th of this month at our lawyer's office."

Babu and his aides came on that date with the money, and the agreement was signed by both parties. Fifty lakhs in cash and fifty lakhs in demand draft. Divya came with the lawyer to our office and submitted the cash and DD. I threw a plane ticket on the table.

"Take this and that DD and leave. Now, you will be handling our Kerala office. The 50 lakhs is your loyalty bonus." Divya was ecstatic. She hugged Ghoush and kissed him. When she realised she was in my office, she quickly thanked me and left.

"Khan! What is happening between you two?"

"Nothing, bhai." He was blushing.

"When did all this start?"

"Couple of months ago, bhai. You were in Kerala and we were working late. We got chatting and one lead to another and..."

"Is this just a time pass for you?"

"No bhai, I am serious about her. We wanted to tell you and then settle down, but I told her to wait for some more time as we need to finish some unsettled accounts. When you asked her to help, she jumped at the occasion, knowing that we could get married soon."

"Rascal, all this behind my back! Congrats! She is a nice girl. Go and help her pack and drop her at the airport."

The next day, the front page of the newspaper carried a story on how the anti-corruption wing, laid a trap on the 26th for Kottunur Inspector Harish, and he was caught red-handed for accepting a bribe and was suspended immediately. Ghoush had approached him on my instructions for help with clearing one of our own offices. He had demanded Rs. 25,000 in cash, after which his team of goons would clear the place. This information we passed to the corruption wing. Harish was suspended with immediate effect. I knew that he would buy his way back into the system; before he did so, my old friend ACP Gupta moved into action and got an inspector from his team into the post at Kottunur station.

We sent our boys to build a wall around the farm that I had brought. As expected, Babu and his boys turned up there.

"What the hell is going on here? This is my land now! I have the sale agreement here!" Babu screamed as his boys removed sticks from the car and started chasing our labourers off the land.

"Anna, wait. Our boss is on the way. There must be some confusion," one of the boys told him. Strict instructions were given to our boys not to harm Babu in any way.

"Why should I wait? All of you leave immediately!" He kept trying to call Divya's number. That was disconnected the day she had left.

Soon, we pulled up in my Mercedes. When Babu saw us, he went into a state of shock. I walked up to him and punched him in the face.

"Kya, Babu, remember me?" His people recognised us and began to run, but our boys chased them down. I went to the car and took out a hockey stick. "Babu, this is my land. Divya was my secretary. She has registered the land in my name. You are trespassing in my property with intent of violence."

I took the hockey stick and began to beat Babu and his men until my arms began to hurt. I gave the stick to Ghoush Khan and told him to continue. I took out a hanky and wiped the sweat off my face.

"Bhai, if we hit them anymore, they will die," Khan said.

"Take this fellow to the station," I told him. My shirt and pants were spattered with drops of blood. At the station, since the Inspector was our man, a case of trespassing with intent to rob and hurt and cause damage was filed. Instructions had been given to file cases against everybody expect Babu. After getting medical attention, the men were shifted back to the station. All except Babu. When they asked Babu why they getting arrested and he was not, he himself was shocked. "I will get bail for all of you," he told them.

In the jeep, the constables were told to talk about how Babu had called the higher-ups and managed to escape, thus leaving the others behind. Meanwhile, when Babu got home, there was an income tax raid in his house. ACP Gupta's old classmate was now the commissioner of income tax, and they were following Babu from the time he had spoken to Divya about the land deal, and the required amounts in black and white. They traced the lockers where he had hidden his ill-gotten wealth. His money was taken away and he was given a notice to come to the office for further clarification. After they left, I drove up to his house. On seeing me, he froze. I sat on a chair in front of him and lit a cigarette.

"The tax people were sent by me. Your people are in jail because of me. You are a pauper because of me. Your properties are attached and seized because of me. Your bank accounts are frozen because of me."

He fell to his knees and began to weep. "Bhai, please forgive me. I am sorry!"

"I will, but you will have to help me."

"How can I help, bhai? Tell me, I will definitely do whatever I can!"

"I need details about Ramesh – where he goes, what he does, where his money is stacked...who, what, everything. If I find something useful, I will let you go."

12. Revenge

I had not spoken to my family for years, and there was little contact from their side. I sometimes wondered how they were. I heard from Ghoush that Dev had begun to work in a company called Eagles Event Management Company in Hennur, but he never called or visited me. Dad visited me once in a while without anyone else's knowledge. I told him my plans for taking down Ramesh.

"Son, today you have power and money, so you will take your revenge. Tomorrow, they will have the same and will seek out revenge. This keeps going on till one gives up."

"Dad, revenge is all I have.Don't take that away from me."

He was disappointed but kept it to himself. If mom called, he would tell her he had gone out for a walk.

Babu began to feed us information. Ramesh had two sons – Anup and Vijay. Vijay had an MBA from Columbia University and ran the engineering college and all the white-collar firms. Anup dealt with government contracts, land acquisitions, construction and so on. Both were in a financially better position than me.

"Bhai, Babu was easy to handle, but those two fellows will be a bit difficult," said Ghoush.

"Difficult! We didn't have one rupee in our pocket before we started this business – now look where we have reached! You don't need power and money to break them. We need brains and a little bit of patience."

Our boys began to track their family.

"Bhai, Anup and Vijay do not get along...they keep fighting about everything. Since Ramesh is not well, the fighting has become more evident. One bad news: the company that Dev is working in belongs to Vijay," said Ghoush.

"What! Call Dev immediately and give me the phone."

Ghoush called Dev.

"Dev, do you know who you working for?" I asked him.

"Yes, I do...What is your problem now?"

"His father is the same person that was trying to grab our land."

"Yes, I know. He met me. Those are things of the past. How do they matter now?"

"I don't know how you can work for someone who tried to cheat your father and beat up your brother."

"Mom and dad are aware of whom I work for, and they have no problems." He ended the call.

"Get me complete information on Anup as soon as possible," I told Khan.

Anup was a gambler, a womaniser and one step away from becoming a full-blown alcoholic. I decided to meet him at one of his gambling dens in Goa, which he frequently visited. We entered the Casino Royal and sat at the table where he was playing. The game was three cards or teen patti. Ghoush brought my chips and placed it in front of me. I continued to play and always played blind (I did not open my cards). I did not see my cards even though, after the third round of betting, you are allowed to see your cards and cannot play blind.

"Boss, you can see your cards now," Anup told me.

"Yeah, I know, but I choose not to."

Some games I won, some I lost. Soon, everyone else left, and only Anup and I where left at the table.

"Mister..." he asked.

"Aryan."

"Hi, I am Anup."

I nodded.

"Do you mind telling me why you don't pick up your cards to see your hand before betting?"

"Anup, what's the point of gambling? The entire thrill goes the moment you know what cards you are holding. The actual thrill lies in opening your cards along with opponents and seeing who won. How about one last game?"

"Sure."

He dealt the cards and we began betting after the fourth round. I asked for a show of cards. He had two sevens and a king. I picked up my cards and saw them, and looked disappointed. He laughed and began pulling the chips towards himself. I placed my cards down and got up.

"Boss, why don't you join me for a drink?" he asked.

"Sure."

He gathered his chips; Ghoush gathered mine. Anup and I made for the exit. I saw Ghoush lifting up my cards to see my hand. He turned to me; I winked at him. He understood. I had three nines.

We followed Anup's car till we reached his hotel. He had booked the penthouse. We entered the living room, where we saw a girl dressed in her bathrobe, watching TV.

"You, move to the bedroom and get dressed," Anup told her. He poured me a drink.

"So Mr. Aryan, what do you do?"

"We are into lots of business."

"Like?"

"We deal with money management, corporate land banking and so on for foreign companies."

"So, you help foreign companies set up business in India."

"We finance them here in India and collect the money in their country for a small commission."

"Hawala, right?"

"Walls have ears..." I replied. "What about you, Anup? What do you do to deserve such a beautiful pent house and a beautiful girlfriend?"

"Ha ha ha...She is not my girlfriend..."

"Okay, so what do you do?"

"We run an engineering college, real estate and we have two small companies dealing with events and IT solutions."

"Superb! So you are running an engineering college?"

"Yes, my family does."

"Which one, may I ask?"

"CERIT: Chikk Eswarappa Reddy Institute of Technology in Bangalore," he replied.

"Doesn't that belong to Mr. Vijay?"

Anup replied in an irritated voice, "He is my younger brother."

"Oh I see. I never saw you in that college before, that's why I asked."

"He is handling the college. How do you know my brother? What business do you have with Vijay?"

"Anup, I deal with transfer of money from here to there and there to here. You understand what I mean." I knew I had installed a seed of doubt in his mind against his own brother. "So, you are handling real estate and the other two companies?"

"No! Vijay is handling the companies...I am into real estate," Anup replied in a loud voice.

"Ok, ok. Calm down."

"Sorry Aryan, just tired...you know how it is..."

"You are bugged because your brother is handling the entire prime portfolio?"

He twitched and gulped his drink. "I hate him; he sucked up to my father and got everything under his control."

"I understand how you feel," I said and poured him another drink. He was feeling guilty about pouring out his feelings to a complete stranger. To ease the tension, I spoke about the different casinos in Goa. Soon, it was morning. We said our goodbyes and I left the room. While walking towards the lift, Anup came running towards me. "Why did you need to meet Vijay in the college?" he asked me.

"Let's take some rest and meet in the evening at my hotel at 7," I said.

"Which one?"

"At The Leela. The maharaja suite, under the name David."

"Ok. See you later."

When he came to the hotel, I asked Ghoush to keep him waiting. After some time, I came out of my room and apologised for the wait.

"Let me get you a drink," I said and began to pour him a drink.

"Yesterday, you told me that you met my younger brother Vijay..."

"Yes, regarding some work he had with me," I replied.

"May I know what work it was?"

"Sorry, I can't tell you. It's client privacy."

"I understand, but why does he need to meet a person who launders money for a living."

"Anup, I think you need to watch your mouth," I said in a raised tone

"Sorry boss, I didn't mean to question you. I was wondering if he is siphoning money away from the college. Before dad makes any decision or passes away..."

"Why don't you ask him yourself?"

"He won't tell me," he said and looked down.

"He gave us two million US dollars and we submitted that same amount in his Swiss account. Now, normally, this all is confidential, but I have a feeling we can do business together."

"Two million US? When did he start a Swiss account?"

"I just gave you such important news and this is how you react?" I spoke harshly.

"Sorry boss, I was just wondering...Thanks for the information. But what can I do if my father favours him?"

"There are many things that can be done. I will help you get what is yours, but what will I get in return?"

"Anything, boss."

"Shares and a post in the board of directors of your group. It will help me keep a clean image, and I will always be one vote you can always count on." He pondered for a while, trying to act as though he was thinking, but I knew his answer before he did.

"Done. But how we do we remove Vijay from the chairman's post?"

"That, I will tell you when the time comes. Now, let's enjoy our drinks and go out and see this beautiful town. After all, we are here to enjoy!"

Anup was hooked.

In Bangalore, Anup came to my farmhouse and gave me more details about his group, its investments and how much money the group was making.

"Anup, from what you tell me, the college is your main business and backbone for all your other companies," I said.

"Yes."

"So, it looks like we need to break that first."

"But that will affect me as well!"

"You are just a board member. For you to get to the chairman's post, I need to break your group's backbone, and you need to fix it."

"How do we do that, bhai?"

"Ghoush, book two tickets to Kerala."

He booked three; he was not letting me out of his sight. In Kerala, I went to see the old man who had helped us with the dollar currency case.

"Aryan beta!"

"Old man...still going strong..." I said as I hugged him.

"Ha ha ha...Who is this new character?" He knew Ghoush; he was asking about Anup. "Come, sit down..."

"I need engineering certificates of a particular college," I told him.

"What? Such a small request?"

"I need thousands of them, spread over the last four years."

"Thousands!" The old man was shocked.

I turned to Anup. "How long has Vijay been in the chairman's post?"

"Four to five years," he replied.

"Spread them across four years. Ghoush will give you the names and other details," I said.

"Aryan, the police will trace you out soon. So, do it slowly over a period of time," the old man warned me.

"Don't worry. I want the police to find out, but you have my word that nothing will reach your doorstep," I told him.

Soon, all our offices in south India were contacted and informed that they should start taking details of people who needed original engineering certificates and job recommendation letters. A rate of Rs. 75,000 was set per package. We had 1,853 applicants – total collection would be approximately 14 crores, with one crore from that set aside for the old man. This was our last deal in the duplicate application field. This was the last haul. After this, severance would be paid and the employees would be asked to relocate, as there were chances of the police tracing them. Vinod from our group agreed to be the front man. If the investigations were not carried out in a controlled manner, the entire operation would go haywire. So, I decided to leak the information to my old friend and newly promoted DCP, Gupta, and his team. Once he was on board, we could control the entire show. Vinod's family would be well taken care of.

We collected the money and distributed the report cards and fake employment letters for all 1,853 applicants. After they received jobs, we gave the leads to DCP Gupta and team. They caught Vinod and confiscated the fake certificates. Every certificate was issued from CERIT College. Before all this started, Vinod was made to call Vijay's cell number every alternate day from his very own mobile number. This established that Vinod and Vijay had been chatting. We also took photos of Vinod sitting behind Vijay at a coffee shop. This was more than enough for us to get our work done – we did not want to shut down the college, only remove Vijay from the board.

Soon, everything went into execution mode. The old man was so busy with our work, he refused other jobs. Ghoush stayed back to ensure proper execution, as this was in another state. I flew back with Anup. A month after all the collections were made and payments were received, Anup showed me his offices. We started with the companies he owned, which were housed in a building next to the college. It was Eagles, the one Dev was working in.

"Boss, this is our company."

"Soon to be run by my friend...Anup," I said.

"All thanks to you, boss."

Coffee was served. An assistant came in, asking for his signature on some files.

"Anup, you finish your work. I will be on the terrace having a smoke."

"Feel free, boss; it's your office."

I went to the terrace and enjoyed a cigarette. After I finished, I began to wander around the office, seeing the setup that I intended to ruin. As I was walking around, I stood outside a cabin. Some meeting was going on inside. Dev was in the meeting. He had grown up from the last time I saw him, which was years back. I saw him through the glass partition. He saw me staring at him. After a couple of seconds, when his expression changed, I realised he had recognised me.

"Boss, where were you? I was looking all over for you?" Anup said as he placed his hand on my shoulder.

"I was just wandering around," I replied, still looking at Dev.

"Come, my work is over. Let's get a drink."

Later that evening, Dev came to my residence to meet me.

"Why did you come to office today? How do you know Anup?"He asked me

"You have come to see me after so many years, and these are the questions you ask me?"

"I know you are up to something. I will inform Vijay."

"You inform whoever you want to."

"Can't you let the past be in the past? Why do you always have to do something about everything? I have just about begun to settle down in life and work hard to make a name for myself. You want to ruin this for me?"

"Not you. I was humiliated. I was beaten up. I faced their father and his friends while you attended college and drank. I fought and won the case...I spent ten days in the hospital...Don't you dare come into my house and ask me to let the past be the past. That past has decided what my future will be. Because of that land, I lost my friends, I lost my love, and I lost my family. Most of all, I lost my respect..."

He turned and left. I was in tears. On his way down the stairs, he met Ghoush Khan.

"Dev, you should be with your brother on this," Khan told him.

"Who the hell are you to tell me what to do and what not to do?"

"I am nobody to you, but your brother is like an elder brother to me."

"Good for you. Go, be with him."

"You remember your little run-in with the police few years ago? Your drunken friends and you beat up a policeman's son, who eventually went into a comma?"

"How do you know about that?"

"What did you think? That, after you got arrested, they let you out for good behaviour? Your elder brother came to know about your situation. He called me and asked me to own up to the crime as he was out of station."

"What?"

"Yes, I took the blame for your crime. It is because of your brother you are roaming a free man."

Dev left the house.

The next day, the newspaper published a report on report card scam, and all regional TV channels covered the topic. During investigation, it was found out that all certificates were issued in the name of CERIT College of Engineering. By evening, they were at Vijay's doorstep. As the chairman of the college, he was taken in for questioning.

A few days later, a board meeting was called. Everyone asked for Vijay's resignation from that post and proposed Anup in his place. Anup was voted in as chairman. He called me with the good news.

"My job is done. What about your end of the deal?" I asked him.

"Boss, give me some time. I just got elected."

"It's ok...Are you going to the hospital to see your father?"

"No, I am not going."

"You should go and announce the good news to him."

"For him, this is bad news. Anyway, you are probably right. I will go and meet him with the news."

After Anup visited his father in the hospital, I went there to meet my old nemesis. I wanted him to know how I was destroying his family. He could not walk, talk or speak but could hear clearly.

Ghoush entered the room had asked all the attendees to leave. Nobody questioned him. I entered the room after everyone left the room. Ramesh was looking old and weary; his life was hanging by a thread. He woke up from his slumber and gazed at me; his eyes opened wider as he stared at me. I pulled up a chair and sat down, then nodded at Ghoush.

"You dog, come here!" Ghoush shouted and pushed Babu into the room.

Babu entered the room. His face and head were clean-shaven.

"Do you remember this fellow?" I asked Ramesh.

He looked at Babu and then at me.

"He works for me; he has given every detail of your family and your holdings."

Ramesh looked angrily at Babu.

"Slap him, Babu," I said.

Babu walked up to Ramesh hesitantly, and slapped him slowly across the face. I walked up to Babu and struck him hard across his face.

"This is how you slap, asshole. Did you forget how you slapped me? Get out from here!"

I could see Ramesh's eyes well up with tears.

"The story does not end here, old man. Your elder son, who is the new chairman, was put into position because of me and my boys. Now, I will be on the board of directors of the companies that you cheated people and established."

Tears began to fall from his eyes.

"Soon, I will break your company and your family. I will bring them to their knees. You tried breaking my family and me – now, wait and watch what I do to your family. I want you to see how your sons fight over your ill-gotten wealth till they destroy all that you have earned."

It was a real pleasure seeing him cry helplessly. As I walked out, I could see Vijay and Dev walking towards the room.

"Mr. Aryan, I was expecting to see you here. Celebrating early, I suppose...Dev has told me everything already," Vijay said.

I looked at Dev who was trying to hide behind Vijay.

"I won't let you succeed in your plans. What have we done to you? Didn't you get your land back?" asked Vijay.

I tore open my shirt and showed him the scars left from the beating Babu and his henchmen had bestowed upon me on the behest of his father.

"You are just looking at the scar inflicted by your father. Look carefully at how deep the scars run. I will destroy you and your family," I buttoned my shirt and began to walk. I turned back, stared at Dev and muttered, "If only you were not my brother..."

13. Tightening the Noose

Soon, I was inducted into the board as an independent director, even though Vijay opposed the move. Because of the scam, everyone supported Anup and distanced themselves from Vijay.

"Bhai, welcome!" Anup said.

"Thank you."

"Bhai, what about Vijay's money that you had transferred to his Swiss account? Is that still with you or is the deal already done?"

The greedy fellow was not happy that he was the chairman of the company – he was now going after Vijay's supposedly ill-gotten wealth. This guy was more than enough to destroy their family – no wonder his father kept him at bay.

"Enjoy the chair you have now. I will see that all becomes yours very soon, as long as I get my share from everything. By the way, how much is this company worth?" I asked him.

"We will get to know soon. I have called all the directors for a general meeting and asked for a detailed presentation on our holdings from the accounts department," Anup said.

I knew he had set up this meeting to see where the money was coming from, and how he could get his hands on it. Soon, the meeting took place. I was able to understand that the college was not entirely their own – most of the present directors had a stake in the company. Ramesh Reddy's family had the largest part (52 percent). The entire group was made up of seven investors, out of which three were Anup, Vijay and Ramesh Reddy. Others were previously investors, who were now directors. Ramesh has 20 percent; Vijay 16 percent and Anup had 16 percent share in the company. The other directors and investors were Ramesh Reddy's old friends or confidantes. One of the directors was a young chap named Jacob T.; he was the same age as Anup. On further inquiry, we found out that he was the son of Tony Chacko – the same guy who broke our factory wall. Fate was bringing us all together for one final battle. He had a 20 percent stake in the company.

"Anup, do you know how to run a college?" I asked him one day.

"What is there to know? We have hired the best there is to run the college. The major decisions we control. But if I had my way, I would have started a hotel," he replied.

In his answer lay my future plans. How was I going to kick them out of their own company? The group had an engineering college, an event management company, a software business and finance business under its belt. I was inducted as an independent director with no holding in the company. My target was to remove Ramesh Reddy and his family's holding in the group and take over completely.

"You have the money now. Why don't you start the hotel? Put a proposal on the table when the directors meet next time."

"You are right. I keep forgetting that I am chairman and can put this dream of mine into action."

"What type of hotel are you planning?"

"Five-star. I have the entire idea up here, in my head." He said. I really doubted he had anything in his head

"Superb! You can probably add a casino to the hotel." I said

"Yes, that would be awesome! No need to go to Goa if we have our own casino here." He siad

"True. So, work out the proposal and we can put your plans into action."

The next meeting was in a couple of months. My informers kept me updated on how Anup had been meeting with architects and designers. My informers tailed him and Vijay all the time. Meanwhile, I met Jacob at a party.

"Hi." said Jacob

"Hello Jacob.Pleasure seeing you here."

"Same here. Enjoying after a hard day's work?"

"Hard? I don't know. Enjoying, yes! Come, sit at my table."

Soon we got talking about how his father transferred his share of 20 percent before he had passed away due to cancer.

"You are really smart for your age. You see the future and are not stuck in repetitive forms of doing business," I told him. Men who lost their father early in life yearn for such approval.

"Sir, I am also exploring new business ventures."

"Why don't you trying to set up a 5-star hotel?"

"That requires a huge investment."

"Anup is planning to bring that to the board in the next meeting. Back him and you can be second in command to the operation of the hotel."

"Anup? When did he become so hard working?"

"The moment you all made him chairman of the company."

"We had no other option. It had to be someone from that family; we were too scared to stand up to them. I just went with the flow."

This told me two things about Jacob: One, he was spineless; two, he did not like the Reddy family.

A couple of weeks later, Anup presented his glamorous idea at a board meeting. The other directors had made Anup the chairman for the sole reason that there was a case on Vijay's head, and they didn't want any media attention. No one expected Anup to come up with investment plans. So, when asked for a vote on whether they should further research the idea of opening a hotel with a casino, the directors immediately turned down his idea.

I met Anup at his apartment later that evening. He was drunk.

"How dare they turn my proposal down so sharply? There was no room for discussion!" he shouted.

"Relax. Try some other idea."

"What other idea? This is my company! Why should those assholes decide what I should or should not do with my company?"

"Anup, there is no pointing in shouting. As I see it, you have only two options if you are really serious in starting this hotel project. You sell your share to someone,take the money and begin your own firm, or you buy out the majority share in your company. How much do you actually hold?" I asked him innocently.

"Sixteen percent."

"So Vijay and your dad hold the rest of the 52 percent?"

"Yes."

"Why don't you get your dad to transfer his share to you?"

"He can't speak or move. Only after he passes away will I know what he has left behind for me."

"I am so sorry. What if he has left everything to Vijay, or if Vijay has managed to make everything his own?"

His eyes were red. "It is highly possible that the snake would do something like that!"

"You need 52 percent to have complete control over your company. Now you are just a dummy chairman. Or, sell of your share and start the hotel in which you will be independent of all these people."

"Sell? Isn't that letting Vijay win?"

"Win! Ha ha ha. Sell your share and start your hotel project. Remember, as a son, you are entitled to half of your father's share. So, technically, you will still be a part of the group once your father passes away. With the revenue from the hotel, you can buy back your share and more."

"Bhai, that's a wonderful idea! Wait...but who will buy my share?"

"Leave that to me. After all, I am your friend."

A couple of days later, I called upon my old friend Gomes to be the front man. I scheduled a meeting between Anup and Gomes.

"Hi Aryan, long time, no see. Where you been? Here or Switzerland?" Gomes asked.

"Here sir, helping out my friend," I replied and introduced Anup.

They shook hands and sat down. Gomes's auditor came forward and introduced himself and began explaining his valuation. He came out with a figure for Anup's share – 11 crores. At this point, Anup interjected: "What? 11 crores? Are you kidding me?"

"Mr. Anup, your group has some history of illegal transaction. Plus, the recent controversy stands to bring down your valuation. The net growth profit has also come down steadily for the past three years," the auditor replied.

"My share alone is worth 20 cores. You have undervalued it," Anup said.

"Mr. Anup, I came here to help you because Aryan called for help. I have no interest in your company. In fact, I will transfer the entire ownership of what I buy to Aryan. Whenever you ready to pay back the amount with interest, you can take back your share. I am ready to put in 11 crores, which is the valuation according to my auditor. Take it or leave it," Gomes said firmly.

"Gomes ji, please give us a minute to discuss," I asked Anup to follow me to the other room.

"Bhai, he is underquoting the value," Anup told me as soon as we reached the room.

"No one is going to buy into your dying company. He is also willing to sell it back to you later. If someone buys at your value and company grows, what guarantee that he will sell it back to you?"

"But the hotel project's land and construction will cost at least 20 crores."

"What are the banks for? But you take a call. I am only helping you out."

"Can't he just give us the 11 crores as loan instead of taking the share?"

"Would you do that if you where in his position?"

After thinking for a bit, Anup agreed. Soon, the papers were drawn up and the board of directors and investors were informed. Everyone was waiting for Anup to get out of their way – all except Vijay, but he had to succumb to the board's vote. Soon, the shares were transferred to me. Now I owned 16 percent of Ramesh Reddy's company. It was time to get hold of more shares to have a majority in the company. If father and son joined hands, they would still be in the majority with 36 percent.

I needed Jacob's help to get on board with Anup's hotel plans so that I could buy out his share too. I didn't have the money to go forward with my plan, as the entire money that Gomes actually put forward was my savings – he had just helped me out by being the front man for the deal. How could I get hold of Jacob's share? He was not desperate, and was not going to let go of his shares for a lesser value.

"Bhai, can't you borrow money?" asked Ghoush.

"Ghoush, when you don't have grey matter, why do you talk?" I replied, irritated. "We require 20 crores. Who is going to give it to me?"

"Sorry, I was just trying to help."

I walked up to the window and lit a smoke. I saw out from the window that an auto had come in front of the gate. Dad stepped out. The security guard quickly paid the auto fellow and opened the gate for him. Dad came upstairs and wished me: "Happy Birthday, my son." I had forgotten that it was my birthday.

"Here is your gift." He took out a bottle of Jack Daniels.

Ghoush got the glasses and ice. I was still thinking about how I would get the money to gain the controlling share into the company.

"What happened? Aryan, you look worried." dad said.

"Nothing. Just business matters."

"Trying to think how to get complete control of the company right? I came to know the day you managed to buy out one son's share. Your brother told us." He took a sip. "Now you own 16 percent, but you think you need the majority to control the company. Right?"

"Yes."

"Relax, it will happen. It is your birthday. Learn to enjoy life; don't let it pass you by."

"Dad, come with me. I have a gift for you. I was planning on giving it to you later, but I think today is a good time. Khan, start the car."

"Where are we going?" Dad asked me.

"That's a surprise!"

Khan was at the driver's wheel. "Where to, bhai?"

"Factory."

After I said this, Khan picked up his phone and called someone. "Keep him ready. We are coming there soon," he said to someone on the other side of the phone.

After an hour, we reached the Capco Blocks factory.

Dad looked at me. "What's going on here?" he asked.

"Come in, dad. I will explain everything inside."

This was the place where we had once gone to sell dad's old machines. As we looked at our old machine lying there, rusted and worn out, Khan went inside and informed the receptionists that we had come to meet Mr. Arun.

"Bhai, he has come out from his office," Ghoush whispered in my ear. I turned around and saw him walking towards us.

"To what do I owe the pleasure of this visit?"

"I think you need to sit down before I tell you," I replied.

He directed us towards his office. "Yes, tell me," he said.

"Do you remember me? Or this man here?" I asked.

"No." Dad had lost most of his hair and I had grown a beard.

"This man is Mr. Dutt – the owner of scrap machines you bought, which are lying out there. I am his son, who sold them to you."

"Yes, I remember that arrogant young man. How I can help? Have you come to buy the scrap back?" He had a smirk on his face.

"No, I have come to buy your factory." The smirk was wiped off his face. Dad was also shocked.

"What the hell are you talking about?" he shouted.

"I am talking about buying your dying company."

"What do you mean by dying company?"He asked quveringly

"Firstly, your sales have dropped by 70 percent in the last year because of the block factories that were opened up beside you. Secondly, you have begun to default on your loan payments. We know the bank has sent you a final notice. So, you either sell the factory to me or I will buy it from the bank."

There was silence. Then he spoke slowly, "What...why... How did you know?"

"The factories in the neighbourhood were set up by my people and we are selling at a profit margin you can never compete with. Profit was not the reason we opened the factory. It was a matter of time before you folded your cards."

"But why? What harm have I done to you or your father? Didn't I help you at your time of need?"

"You didn't help. You brought those machines to boost your ego and pride. They are still out there on display – that shows that your pride and ego are intact."

"Yes, I bought it from you because of my pride, but I was not the reason for your factory shutting down. Why are you showing your anger over your father's failure on me?" Arun asked me.

"Aryan, whatever this man might have done, does not justify what you are doing to him. He was not the reason for our factory to shut down. It was my bad health and lack of business," dad added.

"Khan, bring that fellow inside," I said. Khan went out and brought in an elderly fellow. Dad turned around and exclaimed, "Naryan! What are you doing here?"

"Mr. Arun, will you explain everything or do you want me to explain?" I stared at him. He knew he was caught.

"Dad, this supervisor of yours was passing of all your clients' details to Capco Blocks. When you were not around, if any client called for blocks, he would inform them you were out of stock and that they should call Capco. The two of them made you lose your business."

Dad looked down in disappointment and said, "Naryan, I took you into the company when you had no place to sleep or food to eat. I taught you the job, and paid for all your expenses. Why did you do this to me? Do you know what happened to my family because of your greed? Aryan, please take him away." Dad began to cry. I nodded and Khan pushed Naryan out.

"Aryan, how did you find out about this?" dad asked.

"Dad, Naryan not only brought the deal for getting our machines sold, he also cleverly made his friend the broker from Capco blocks. While we where shifting the machines into the truck, I overheard them speaking. Naryan was giving him instructions on what to do and what not to do. I still went ahead because we were in need of money. Soon after the deal ended, I began to inquire with the other workers and found out what actually happened."

Dad turned to Arun, "You have spoilt my life and my son's life! Buy this factory, Aryan! And bring this fellow down to where he belongs!"

Dad turned and walked out. I followed him, but turned back at the door to say one last thing: "The bank manager is a friend of mine, so don't expect any grace from him. I will be buying your company one way or the other."

Soon, at the bank auction, I brought the factory in dad's name.

14. Belekari Port

Mr. Gomes came down from Delhi to meet me. The DCP had fixed a meeting. I knew it was something dangerous – if not, they would not have called on me. We met at The Ramada Hotel. We exchanged a few pleasantries and began to drink. Soon, Gomes began the real conversation. "Aryan, we need your help."

"How can I be of service?"

"We need you to help us with transportation."

"Transportation of what?"

"My partner has gotten into the mining business in Bellary. We are only allowed 16 tonnes per load, and there is a restriction on permitted loads allowed. We have encroached on the neighbouring forests and the output is greatly increased. We need someone to take the extra load from us and deliver to Belekari Port."

"So, the trucks are mine, and the risk of plying between Bellary and Belekari Port is all mine. Once the load reaches the port, it is all yours."

"Yes."

"How many loads are going out per day now?"

"Four hundred loads at 16 tonnes per load for a two axel truck," the DCP replied.

"How much more per day do you expect?"

"We require you to do a minimum of 3,000 loads per week – that is 48,000 tonnes per week."

"Payment?"

"Weekly payout at Rs. 900 per tonne." Gomes replied.

"So, about Rs. 14,400 per load?" I confirmed. "I need you to increase the rate as all transport risk is mine and the vehicles cost is also mine. Plus, I need a daily payout. This is illegal stuff. The moment the truck hits the port area, you must cash us out."

"I need to discuss this with my partner," So saying, Gomes stepped into the bedroom to make the call.

I turned to the DCP and asked him, "Sir, do you think this is possible? Won't there be a police check post and the mining department's check post?"

"Aryan, it's not easy, but I am sure you will come up with something. The permits are issued by the department of mines and geology, and also by the forest department in leases given in forestland – these are called mineral dispatch permit or MDP. Along with the MDP, a trip sheet is a must. Trip sheets are issued for each lorry. The first check will be done by the department of mining regarding weight and load trip, which needs to be entered into the system – without this, your vehicle could be seized. You will have to cross two major check posts before reaching your destination. There is also an occasional surprise check done by the RTO. But, if done right, you will be doing business to the tune of five crores a week," the DCP replied.

That was a lot of money, but I would only get a portion of that amount, as I would have to grease or arm-twist a lot of people to remove kinks in the operations. This could be my ticket to buying a controlling share in the Eagle Group.

My line of thought was broken when Gomes came back into the room.

"Aryan, if you are free, we need to do a trip to Bellary. My partner has asked you to come and see our operation, and discuss it further with him."

So we went to Bellary. We reached a huge white mansion with guards posted all around the building. When we entered into the building, we were patted down by the guards. Even Gomes was checked. Then, we were ushered into a living room, which was filled with artifacts from around the world. What caught my eye was a black panther sculpted out of a single piece of black stone. I walked up to it and examined it. It was really beautiful; I wanted it.

"That is my priced piece. I got it from London at an auction. Paid half a million Euros for it."

I turned and saw a man dressed in white and wearing lot of gold jewellery come down the marble staircase. He went up to Gomes and hugged him. Gomes introduced us: " Aryan, meet Somashekar."

"Hi, Aryan."

"Hello Mr. Somashekar."

I could some feel the tension in the room when I called him by his first name. He laughed and said, "Come, sit down. Let's have tea."

Snacks and tea were served; it was enough food to feed a village.

"So, has Gomes filled you up on our requirements?"

"Yes, he has."

"Any questions or doubts?" he asked me.

"Yes, I have two points. I need payouts the moment my trucks hit your stockyard; and the rates have to be increased."

"You are only bothered about that? No questions as to why, who, what?"

"Mr. Somashekar..."

"Call me Soma."

"Soma, you need iron ore to be shifted from your mines, above the permitted loads sanctioned by the government. Also, you need ore to be shifted from your illegal patta lands without any records on paper – for which you need an outside person's help. So, here I am. The only thing that should concern me is shifting your materials from Bellary to Belikari Port safely. The only concern you should have is about making my payments on time."

He gazed at me for a few seconds and then stood up.

"Gomes, close it with him on his terms. You are probably the only fellow who is walking out of here with all your terms and conditions. It is probably because I like the way you deal. Let me know once you are ready to start."

He got up and shook hands with me. Soon, we left Bellary and drove back to Bangalore.

Once I reached Bangalore, I met Ghoush Khan and filled him in on the details. Our biggest problem was that we did not have any trucks. I told Ghoush Khan to call all his friends in the moneylending business, and check our own records, to find out which transport company was in complete debt and the number of vehicles they had.

Soon, we had a list of people to examine. Six of them were willing, so long as I gave them a share and a guarantee that their trucks would not be seized. We managed to arrange for a thousand trucks.

"Bhai, we need another 500 trucks," Khan said.

"No, just load these trucks with 24 tonnes each. That way, we only risk 1,000 trucks. The distance to be covered is about 300 km. So, each truck has to do two trips a week. That is a thousand trips at 24 tonnes a trip – so, we achieve 48,000 tonnes. Ask the DCP to come home this evening. Tell him we have arranged for a party for him."

When the DCP came home, we sat down, drank and chatted about old times. Then, he asked, "So, Aryan, what do I owe this invitation to?"

"Sir, we need your help on the deal that we are running for Gomes and Soma."

"You need the traffic-in-charge of the route you are taking?"

"No, sir. I have worked out a chart in which everyone from the constable to the SP gets paid. They will turn a blind eye towards my trucks, which will carry a special printed pass. The money will be given to them at the end of each month."

"You are planning to bribe the entire staff?"

"Sir, I can't have one nosy constable creating unwanted problems for the entire operation. With monthly payments, I will also save a lot of money. My question is, can it be done?"

"Do you have the amount you plan to pay and to whom?"

"Yes. Khan, give him the chart."

As the DCP looked at the chart, Khan refilled our glasses.

"I have a young Inspector in my team...I will transfer him to your route. He will manage your entire payout system. He is quite a capable young chap."

"Sir, thanks, but let him handle the payouts with the cops and officials only. I have teams in place for other payments."

"Why Aryan? Lost trust in us?" he asked with a smile on his face.

"Nothing like that, sir. From that amount, the truck owner also needs to get paid and the officers of the forest department, mining department, and so on."

Soon, the plan was set in motion. Every officer in all the related departments was bought off. Those who stood against us were soon transferred, and the wheels began to move smoothly. Political leaders soon came to us, asking for their cut. We didn't pay them but went straight to their party leaders and paid the top rung, so that the rest would keep quiet.

From time to time, there were small incidents, but they were solved with money or muscle. Soon, I was spending lot of time in Soma's hometown. He had grown fond of me, and we spent a lot of time thinking of new business deals.

One day, he sent someone to fetch me from the apartment I had set up in Bellary. When I reached his house, he said, "Aryan, a proposal has come to me."

"Which new business are you planning to embark on now?"

"Politics."

"What?"

"Yes, my boy. Politics! Where my illegal will also become legal!"

"Soma bhai, I think you are making a big mistake here."

"Why Aryan? Don't you think it is a smart move? Not a single politician has been convicted till date. For people like me, this is the best cover."

"Soma bhai, very few people know what we are doing out here. Once you join politics, your rivals in that field will begin to dig out your history from here."

"Nobody will dare such foolishness! Once we win, we can ask for any prime portfolio that we want to handle."

"Soma bhai, I have always thought that politicians and bureaucrats should work for us. As long as we feed them, there will be no trouble. With this stunt, you will get unwanted media coverage. That is bad for business."

"You worry too much. Nothing is going to happen."

One week later, Soma submitted his nomination to contest in the Lok Sabha elections. I went to his house and congratulated him. However, we both knew that we could not work together anymore – in this world, you follow your friends into the depths of hell or part ways; you can't be a bystander.

Soon enough, as I had expected; he began to muscle me out of my own operations. I used my police contacts and seized his entire consignment. Not long after, a meeting was set up to discuss and settle our issues. The meeting was attended by Gomes, the DCP, Soma and his brother, Ghoush and me.

Gomes said, "Aryan, what you did was wrong."

"Gomes, you tell me I am wrong, but you and you partner go behind my back and start sending loads without using my lorries but by using special passes made by me. Where will I make my living?"

"Hey ass! It is our consignment, our mines; you are just someone we hired to do transport for us!" This was Soma's brother. At this point, Ghoush jumped up, smashed a bottle and lodged it close to his neck.

"Bhai, tell me to do it!" he shouted.

"Ghoush, put it away and sit down," I said sharply. Ghoush sat down but kept the bottle stub in his hands. "Soma bhai, if I or anyone else offended you, we are sorry. I guess we cannot work together anymore. As a gesture of goodwill, I will hand over my entire operations to you and move out from here."

"Aryan, I treated you as family, but you treated this as a business," Soma finally said.

"Soma bhai, it has and always will be only business – I never do business with family. Let me close all accounts with my people, and the contacts will be handed over to your brother. I wish you best of luck in all future endeavours."

Saying this, I got up and signalled to Ghoush to open the door. We walked out and went into the car. In the car, I punched Ghoush in the face; his nose broke and he began to bleed. He didn't ask me anything. He just took out a napkin wiped the blood off his face. He knew that his attack on Soma's brother would have had fatal consequences for both of us, had it not been for my offer of surrender. What he didn't know was that, with Soma's entry into politics, there was a storm brewing – and I knew it was going to hit soon. Soma's move to politics was going to bring down the entire operation, and I wanted out anyway. I had made enough money to get back to my main agenda.

Soon, I shifted back to Bangalore and began concentrating on my work. One day, Ghoush came up to me with my phone and said, "Sahail is on the line," he sounded surprised.

I took the phone from him and listened to Sahail. Finally, I said, "Go ahead and finish the deal soon."

Ghoush Khan was waiting for me to hang up. "Bhai, you are still in touch with Sahail? You did not tell me anything!"

"It's for your own good. Don't worry – the time will come when you will know everything. For now, concentrate on Anup and his hotel dreams." He was to ensure that the hotel did not come up.

My focus was on bringing the rest of the Reddy family to their knees – for that, I needed to break Vijay. He was already under inquiry for the fake certificates, but was clearing his name by using his influence and money power. I needed to hit him and the family hard. Money held that family together – once it was all gone, I was sure they would be at each other's throats. Now, I had the money and needed to increase my stake in the company.

I had a private discussion with Jacob Chacko the present chairman of the company and made him an offer. He agreed to sell his share – soon, all formalities were completed and I owned 36 percent of the company. With that move, I became the largest single shareholder in the company. The Reddy family's stake was left Vijay with 16 percent and his father with 20 percent.

I called Anup to my new office for a meeting.

"Good morning, Anup."

"Yeah. Good morning."He answered with a disgruntled look

"What happened, Anup? You angry or something?"

"Vijay told me everything. Now, you brought out Jacob's share also. That asshole's father worked for my father, but he suddenly jumped ship."

"Didn't you jump first? What this sudden sense of family sentiments?"

"I took your advice sold my share of the business. Now, the hotel business is going bankrupt, and it is not even open yet. The government has buried me with notices." I knew all that was happening as Ghoush's job was to make sure that the hotel was not built, and that Anup did he receive any loans.

"Anup, you are close to me, despite what Vijay has told you. Let me do you a favour and take the hotel project off your hands. I will pay you five crores. With that, you can start something new."

"Five crores! I spent 11 crores and more. I borrowed at least 3 crores from the bank!"

"Anup, don't take me for a fool. No one gave you a loan, and you did not spend 11 crores on the project. I have details on how many visits you had made to Nepal, Bangkok and Goa and how much you spent on gambling, women and drugs. Take this offer before you go bankrupt for sure."

Anup was shocked. "You are out to destroy us completely, aren't you?"

"Anup, take the offer and get away from here."

"Make it six and you have a deal."

"I am willing to pay you six crores, but you will have to file a claim for half of your father's share since he is ill."

"I can't do that." He repiled

"Remember, once your father dies, if Vijay takes everything for him, you will be fighting this case for a very long time. You won't even have the resources to fight till the end. Now is the time if you want to make some money quickly."

He nodded and stood up. "Draw up the papers and tell me where you want my signature." He went towards the door, then stopped and turned. "I wish my family never crossed your path. Things would have been normal. But remember, this does not end. Tomorrow, someone from my family will come after your. It's a cycle Aryan."

He walked out and shut the door. Ghoush followed him and asked him to stay with us till the deal was completed. My next meeting was with Vijay; we met at a restaurant near the office.

"Vijay, I am going to cut to the chase. I want to buy the rest of your family's shares," I said to him the moment he sat down.

"You know I am not going to let you do that. This is my family business. I will not let you take it away from us," he said. I signalled to Ghoush to bring me a file.

"This is the case that is going to be filed in court tomorrow against your father." When he read through the file, his eyes were wide open with shock.

"You...you..."

"Vijay, calm down. I am giving you a way out of this – to end this right here.

"I will fight this case! I am not giving up this case just like that!" He tore the sheets.

"Ghoush, call him," I said. Dev came into the room.

"Dev, what are you doing here?" Vijay asked him.

"What did you think, Vijay? That I was fighting this alone? My brother was in this from the day he saw me at the office. He came home that evening to fight with me about what I was doing. Before leaving, he had a chat with Ghoush. He came back the next day and begged for forgiveness, and said he was ready to leave the company and join me. I instructed him to stay on and find out where you going and who you are meeting. He did whatever I asked him to do," I replied.

"It looks like I have to teach your entire family a lesson soon!" Vijay said as he stood up to leave.

"I would reconsider that. We know about your little secret, Vijay. The reason you keep going to Mumbai?" I said.

Vijay collapsed onto the sofa.

"How? Dev, did you...?" Vijay asked.

"Do you think your family or your business partners will stick around once they know you have a boyfriend in Mumbai?" I asked.

"No one will believe you," Vijay said, gathering some courage.

"Ghoush, call him inside," I said.

A young boy was ushered into the room. Vijay was in shock.

"They got you also?" Vijay asked.

"I need to make a living. I can't be your one night stand for life," he replied.

"I will deny all this! I will fight all of you people!" said Vijay.

"Vijay, don't be stupid. We have photos and videos as proof. Think about your wife and kids – what will they think about the situation you are in right now?" I said.

"So, let's begin. I own 36 percent of the company, and want to buy your family out."

"That's not going happen. You know I am not going to sell."

"Not going to sell? What other option do you have?"

"Okay, even if I sell my share, what about my father's share?"

"Anup is willing to sell his father's share."

"How can he sell what is not his? My father will never agree to sell his share even though he is in his death bed."

"Convince him – if not, both Anup and you have to appeal to the court that your father has gone mad and is not in a position to handle his wealth, and that it has to be transferred to you both. He can't talk, so I don't see him putting up a fight."

"You have really thought things through, haven't you? You have won this round. No need for a case. Just draw up the papers; we will transfer the entire rights in your name."

The brothers signed and collected their respective amounts. I appointed Dev as the chairman of the company; we held a total of 72 percent of the company. I went and visited Ramesh. He looked at me as I walked in.

I went up to his him and whispered into his ear, "I have taken it all."

15. Retribution

We left for Mangalore that very evening. On the flight, Ghoush asked me, "Bhai, why are we rushing to Mangalore? Today is a victorious day for us."

"Ghoush, the victory seems incomplete without the deal we going for," I replied.

"What deal?"

"Close your eyes and rest. We shall be there soon." I picked up the newspaper.

The headline read: *'Somashekar Reddy accused of amassing illegal wealth by means of destroying forest'*. Since his entry into politics, the rival parties had begun to tear down his operations, as they knew he would soon become a threat to their way of life. As I had predicted, the news spread like wildfire.

"They are asking for him to be arrested," Ghoush said, breaking my train of thought.

I smiled. I knew what he didn't – that the power and wealth he had amassed could still be protected if he did just a few years of jail time. I decided I would go and meet him; after all, it was through his business deal that I was able to fulfill my plans.

We checked into a hotel. After a couple of hours, we heard a knock on the door. When Ghoush opened the door, he was shocked. "Sahail!"

Sahail hugged Ghoush Khan, and then walked towards me. I stood up and hugged him.

"Ghoush, fix him a drink too," I said.

"No bhai, no drinks for me," he replied.

"Why? Have you gone back to your old habits?"

"No bhai. I only smoke cigarettes now – only once in a while."

"You look different with the bald head! What happened, Emran Hashmi?" I joked.

"Settled down…I am trying to make a living. When your call came regarding this work, I left everything and came down. Now it's almost done. Once I finish, I will go back to Jammu."

"So, why did you come down?" I asked.

"You call and I don't come? That time you were in hospital, I did not come because of Anjali. She told me not to get involved in it. I listened to her. Some time later, I bumped into Raghuveer from college. He asked me about you. I told him I was not in touch with you anymore.

"He slapped me and told me, 'If it was not for that friend, you would be a druggie like us.' It was already too late; you had moved out of your house and my dad asked me to get back. When I was in Jammu, I thought of contacting you but could not find the courage. When you called and asked for a favour, I dropped everything and came running."

Sahail hugged me once again and said, "Sorry bhai! I truly respect you for what you have done for me!"

"Yaar, stop acting so sentimental. Come, sit down and tell me about the deal."

"We have managed to bring the doctor's clinic to ruin by using those ladies from Mumbai and the cases we piled on his head. He has now taken up a job here in Mangalore JSS Hospital and wants to sell his house and move here."

"Who? What is this deal, bhai?" asked a very confused Ghoush.

"You have not yet told him?" asked Sahail.

"No, I have not; let it be a surprise for him. So, when is the registration?" I asked.

"Tomorrow," Sahail replied.

"Have you stressed on the condition that goes with the agreement?"

"Yes bhai, I got the keys. You can shift there today. Tomorrow, we shall come there after the registration with the original owners to hand over the papers to you."

"No need. I will shift there tomorrow morning; ask some boys to come there for shifting."

"Bhai, what is this long hair and beard? It also looks like you have not slept in ages."

"This is what happens when you spend a lifetime seeking revenge," I replied.

We sat there in silence for a few minutes; then, Sahail excused himself to go meet the lawyer. The next day, we left for Manipal. We stood in front of a big house; the gate had a board with the name '**Dr. Rao**'.

Ghoush still did not understand.